I0628246

ZEN FOOT-NOTES

Bäuu Press

1 2 3 4 5 6 7 8 9 10

Library of Congress Cataloging-in-Publication Data

Omura, Wayne

Zen Foot-Notes: Upon the Unknown Passage /
by Wayne Omura
p. cm.

ISBN 978-1-936955-08-4 (paperback : alk. paper)
1. Fiction. 2. Mountain Climbing 3. Philosophy

The paper in this book meets the guidelines for permanence and durability of the Committee on Production Guidelines for Book Longevity of the Council on Library Resources, Inc.

ZEN FOOT-NOTES

Upon the Unknown Passage

by

Wayne Omura

Bäuu Press

Contents

For the fellow travelers I have met,

and not met, along the path

Tell no one where you are going.

Let no one see you leave.

Simply climb.

Climb,

and never look back.

This is a tale that began long ago . . .

and yet is remembered only now.

This is the journey—

experienced, and then forgotten.

This is the adventure

lost in a dream . . .

DAY ONE

A beginner, hesitant to begin. Am I ready? Have all preparations been made? How much food and water? What kind of clothing and gear? How far and how long and over what type of terrain? I run to and fro setting things in order: map, compass, tools and medicine.

"It doesn't matter," says Tensing, impatiently bursting in upon my work. He appears as he always appears, abruptly and without warning, without regard for my privacy. It is the way of his people—a communal camaraderie. He stands at the entrance, his dirty wool clothing making him a stout bundle, a barrel of rags. But he is our guide on this journey, and we must follow his advice. He tells me to stop planning and worrying. He assures me that the entire journey is a preparation, that everything can be modified and adapted along the way.

"You will grow with each step. You cannot be perfect from day one."

START NOW!

Proceed One Pace Forward

MOBILITY

We are preparing to embark. All possessions are pared to the essential. What is not indispensable is either discarded or given away. Drawers and closets are slowly cleared. Free space is opened. There is room to breathe.

The less one has, the less one has to carry. This whittling away eventually leads to ultimate mobility. One can pick up and leave anywhere, any time. For there is no worry or responsibility for things one does not have.

"Journeying is like preparing to die. One gives everything that cannot be taken."

CARRYING ONE'S WEIGHT

On seeing my pile of bags, packs, and cases of "essentials," Tensing chuckles, strokes his gray beard, and shakes his head.

"I hope you're strong enough to carry all this," he remarks offhandedly. "There will be no porters."

"No porters!" I nearly scream. "But porters are part of every expedition. It's normal. It's traditional. It's essential."

"Essential my foot," says Tensing with a humorous twinkle in his eye. "To succeed on an expedition of this nature it is necessary that each member carry his own weight. Nothing will be gained if someone else carries you up."

DAY TWO

All preparations are finalized. At last we can begin. However, Tensing now tells me that the preparations were themselves simply a part of the journey. "Each movement up to this point has been a necessary part of the trip." Tensing even traces my actions back through childhood to my birth. "You have always been traveling along the way. It is only when you become conscious of it that you begin to falter and eventually stop."

Effortlessly one foot is placed before the other.

A journey of a lifetime begins with one step.

"YOU HAVE ALWAYS BEEN
TRAVELING ALONG THE WAY."

GIVE IT UP

After years of planning and preparation I am stunned that the members of the expedition carry no packs or supplies. They are embarking empty-handed and now I, too, am told to leave everything behind.

"But this is essential," I protest. "I've spent years organizing every detail, every necessity."

However, Tensing is adamant.

"For the moment all that one needs is oneself. All that must be carried is the desire and the will. It must simply be done, here and now. Everything else is just so much extra baggage."

HOME

Point of Rendezvous and Departure

There is much fanfare and jubilation marking the beginning of the journey. The streets are a riot of colorful costumes and decorations. Drinking, carousing, a jovial camaraderie and merrymaking. The festivities pervade every rooftop and cellar. It is a homecoming, a Mardi Gras, a carnival and a parade. But why here, in the midst of comfort and pleasure, do I suddenly have visions of an intense struggle on top? I am happy, yet subdued. For I am no longer a part. In my heart I have already left, abandoning the past, committing myself to the expedition.

It begins subtly, secretly, almost without notice. Such grandeur, such nobility, discernible as only a slight undercurrent, a subliminal manifestation. Off to the side, small groups and advance parties quietly slip away. We are one such group, and this is the story of our departure.

Of course all journeys involve separation and risk, but without separating and taking risks one would never go anywhere.

DESTINATION

At the juncture, Spectacle Taverns, Tensing unravels a tattered scroll upon the scum-laden table. Beer, wine, and grease soak through from beneath. We are surrounded by a throng of rowdy villagers over which Tensing cannot be heard, but there is little to be said. Before us lies the secret map of our journey. All eleven comprising the expedition crowd for a better vantage point. Tensing merely points to a vast, uncharted region. Here Adrian inscribes what Tensing whispers in his ear from above. It is a translation of the strange calligraphy from the top of the page. When Adrian is through, what remains is our goal, our destiny:

Atop Pochen Point, the fabled summit of the nether world, exists one master, one disciple, one teaching, oneself.

FELLOW TRAVELERS

Those who accompany you along the path must be carefully chosen. Each must complement the other, making the whole greater than all of its parts. Companions should not be picked at random, for the weakest link will impede the progress of all. Better to travel alone in the heights than to be dragged down by the burdens of another.

THE CHOSEN

The expedition reaches Devil's Cauldron, a sulphurous hot spring nestled at the mouth of a narrow canyon. We make camp as Tensing scopes out the area. Trivial chatter suddenly turns into heated controversy and suspicion. Somehow it comes out that no one knows anything at all about Tensing. Each claims he heard about Tensing from others. No one acknowledges responsibility for selecting him as our guide. Adrian throws down his gauntlet.

"What kind of trickery is this? No one knows him. He could be a charlatan, a madman!"

"I gave up everything," I say in despair, "everything I never had."

"Now what do we do?" asks Bruce, a young athletic oriental.

"Where do we go?" asks his twin brother, Lee.

Tensing returns to camp seemingly unaware of our suspicion. He moves about doing small tasks until he is forcefully confronted.

"Who are you?"

"Who chose you?"

Tensing is taken aback.

"Chose me?" he says, incredulous. "Me? It was you! It was I who chose you."

HIGHS AND LOWS

Tensing promises to tell his story later. But with darkness falling we must set up camp.

"But why here?" complains Adrian. "It stinks like hell! I can hardly breathe."

"It's the pits," remarks Bruce, pinching his nose with a grimace.

Tensing merely grins and says that this is where we must camp. It is the first test of our obedience. It will determine who commands. Reluctantly, and not without much whining and grumbling, the expedition sets itself up for the night.

Tensing later explains that in order to know the peak, one must first accustom oneself to the pit. In order to appreciate the brisk, clean air on top, one must first be immersed in the foul stench below.

DAY FIVE

"It sure does stink!" bellows Hamel, rousing us to the cold, brisk morning. "But don't it stink lovely?" He growls and yawns and stretches his arms to the crystal-blue sky. We nickname him the Barbarian because of his roughneck manners and burliness. But he is right. With time the stench is only half as bad as the night before. In fact, it has acquired a strangely compelling taste.

A fire is started. Food is prepared. Hamel embarrasses us by doing most of the work. All of us together scarcely do half of what Hamel accomplishes without being asked. In fact, no one would dare ask Hamel for help, because he has done so much already. And he does it so lightheartedly, without the slightest complaint. Having a cheerful "Barbarian" among the expedition keeps everyone on his toes. We are plagued by the guilt that we are not pulling our weight.

Camp is broken, mostly by Hamel, and the expedition moves to its first goal—the Never Summer Mountains.

HARD WORK

The Barbarian's Credo

A challenge. A unification of mind, body, and spirit. To accomplish what needs to be done as quickly as possible, as efficiently as possible. To utilize energy with the least amount of waste. To wield tools expertly with the minimum of excess motion. To flow with the rhythm of work and not go against the grain. To engage wholeheartedly each moment of the most menial task. To become one with work, because hard work strengthens life.

PROCRASTINATED JOURNEYS

At the trailhead to the Never Summer Mountains we come upon a veritable host of small groups and expeditions. People cluster around tables, charts, and billboards with topographic maps. Compasses and binoculars are trained upon the rugged, snowcapped peaks. Although exciting, we quickly grow discouraged by this multitude of fellow-journeyers. Adrian quips that we are no longer unique, for it detracts from our efforts and accomplishments thus far. It is like a tourist attraction, a group anyone can join. Their presence makes our quest commonplace—no longer worthwhile. And yet the enthusiasm and sense of adventure are nevertheless contagious. We can't wait to begin and prove ourselves and our intent.

After several hours of route-planning and finding our bearing, the expedition proceeds along the steep and arduous path into the peaks. Strangely, within moments the crowded noisy landscape is left behind. We find ourselves traveling alone through virtually untrammeled virgin land. To our surprise Tensing explains that this is the way it has always been. "Many plan and elaborate, but never find the impetus to begin. In all the millennia we are one of few to actually start."

THE HIGH ROAD

When coming to a fork along one's path there is a general rule to follow: always take the trail leading to the highest ground. Although the lower trail may be easier no altitude is achieved. Only by strenuous effort can anything worthwhile be gained. Among climbers this is known as: Taking the High Road.

DAY SEVEN

"So," says Lee, panting from behind. "Are we there yet?"

Groans of sympathy and exhaustion chime in from all sides. Hamel chuckles to himself, and yet he is carrying the heaviest pack.

Tensing stops and allows us a rest while he scouts ahead. "But not too long," he admonishes. "Rest only what is needed. Resting longer will drag you down, reminding you of how hard it really is. Don't think of the task and suddenly it is done. Forget the effort and all is effortless."

ACCEPTANCE

     Along every trail lies some sort of difficulty. Every path has its own set of obstacles. Because of this there is no reason to complain, for when all is said and done, one chooses one's own way.

DAY NINE

"My God, aren't you hot? I'm sweating like a pig," I complain.

"I'm freezing!" stammers Adrian. He stands shivering without a coat as a sudden chilling gust sweeps the ridge.

Bruce and Lee are weary from not enough food and water. While others complain of too much food and water weighing their packs. Tensing solves the problem in a most radically unique manner. Adrian receives my wool sweater and mittens. Those who are hungry and thirsty satisfy themselves from the packs of those who are weighed down.

THE BALANCE

A balance must be struck in all aspects of the climb. Too much clothing and you sweat. Too little clothing and you freeze. The same is true for food and water. Too much and they weigh you down. Too little and you cannot make it up. The balance is a fine line upon which ideally one should tread. With water, for example, no more should be taken than will be needed along the way. At the end of the way there should be no water.

THE LONG AND WINDING ROAD

The expedition has become scattered along the mountainside. It has broken up into a segmented pattern, a differentiation I care not to consider. Up ahead, beyond sight, exists Tensing. Is he our scout? Our guide? We don't even know where he is. The only clues are small rock cairns and other trailblazings.

Adrian and Hamel are far ahead, but still within sight. No one else is even close. At times we nearly catch up only to find them darting ahead. The closeness was a frustrating illusion—the existence of a gorge between us down and up which we must tread.

Adrian occasionally turns and watches impatiently from above. I can feel his disdainful glare although all that appears is a tiny, anonymous silhouette. At times Hamel will turn and wave or holler encouragement from above. How do we know it is Hamel? He is the one with the smile.

Bruce, Lee and I follow in a jostling, disgruntled lump. And then far behind are the stragglers—most of whom are not even in sight. I feel sorry, for as things continue, fate will leave them behind.

PACING

Travel as fast or as slow as you please. Do not be frustrated or envious of those who travel faster. Do not be haughty or disdainful towards those who travel slower. When traveling in group, remember that your pace is set by mutual agreement. The situation—slow or fast—was chosen of your own accord. Travel alone rather than complain from your inability to adjust your own pace.

COMPROMISE

On the rim of Flaming Gorge we make camp under a rare Oreodant bush. There is a disturbing silence and tension, an undercurrent of resentment. Eyes are averted, darting and malicious. Everyone is fatigued and unwilling to compromise.

At last it breaks out. "Thanks for waiting," says a straggler sarcastically to his "friend."

"What took you so long? I couldn't stand around forever. I was freezing. Besides, we're supposed to move at our own pace. Why make me feel guilty? If it weren't for you we would have made K-7 by now."

"Well go and make K-7. Let's see you do it alone. We're supposed to be a group, an expedition if you recall."

"Gentlemen, gentlemen," says Tensing in a cheery manner. "It is time for a story. Now gather around beneath the Oreodant and I'll tell you an interesting episode from my life."

I AM ACCEPTED INTO THE ORDER

TENSING'S REVELATION

Tensing prefaces his story with a brief account of his life. He is a member of a secret, esoteric order of Sherpas.

"I thought Sherpas just existed naturally," says Adrian in disbelief.

"Some do," remarks Tensing, "but most have been trained." Many of us around the campfire nod in wonderment. It is what we always suspected, what we always wanted to believe.

"Anyway, back to my story. Shortly after I achieved the level of the black sash, I became assistant to the Head Sherpa and took part in the initiations. These were given twice a year to monitor the student Sherpas' progress and understanding. The initiates would arrive an hour or so before testing. They would study and meditate and practice the rituals and movements."

"What kind of rituals and movements?" asks Adrian. "What kind of rituals and movements do you need to be a Sherpa?"

Tensing is put off by Adrian's badgering. He promises to explain it all later. In fact, he hints that one day he may even perform a "dance." But for now, back to the Sherpas.

"The first initiation I was to preside over left me dumbfounded. A foot of powdered snow had blanketed the monastery grounds overnight. An hour before testing I bundled up in my yak suit, trudged out into the cold morning air, and began clearing the path. Some initiates had already arrived and saw me leave with my shovel. Others arriving from the Sherpas' quarters greeted me and hurried inside. I could understand their anxiety and panic. I had experienced it so many times in the past. I also understood their familiarity with me (after all I used to be one of them) and their unfamiliarity with my new position (I was now one of 'them'). But somehow I felt that they were missing the point.

"The ninth hour was approaching and by now all the initiates had arrived. Through the windows I could see them practicing diligently and frantically inside. At the ninth hour, the time for testing, I had still not finished clearing the path. Something in me stubbornly persisted in seeing it through. Eventually the door opened and a lone, bundled figure approached carrying a shovel. 'Only one,' I thought to myself, wondering who it could be. He set to work on the far side and we gradually worked our way together. What a feeling! The spirit of camaraderie lifted my depression. The initiates were inside the warm training hall, but the two of us outside in the cold would triumph together. We would make it inside in time for the opening ceremony.

    "'No hurry,' said the bundled figure as our cleared path became one. I bowed in astonishment, expecting, at any moment, a reprimand for shirking my duties.

    "'The testing is over,' said the Head Sherpa calmly. 'All initiates have failed. For the real test is this,' he proclaimed, banging his shovel on the stone path. 'The most important test is that of life.' "

    At Flaming Gorge, under the rare Oreodant bush, night flowers open their blossoms to the moon.

THE TEST OF LIFE

The next morning is a miracle. Everyone is up before the crack of dawn. Breakfast is ready within minutes as all pitch in eagerly and good-humoredly outdo one another. Hamel breaks out in raucous laughter as Adrian grabs the axe from his hand and rushes off for the morning firewood. What had formerly taken Hamel a half hour of preparation is accomplished with five minutes of joint effort. In fact, breakfast is over and camp broken before the first light. There is time for a lingering cup of hot yak tea with the rising sun.

HALCYON DAYS

A new phase begins. A group spirit emerges which molds the disparate elements into a whole. All work together in achieving our first objective, K-7—the main obstacle in the Never Summer Mountains on the approach to Pochen Point. The more experienced teach and encourage the less experienced. A whole battery of subtle techniques and wilderness psychology thus ensues.

GOAL SETS

Don't think of what you left behind. And don't think too far ahead. For how can one leave something to which one is tied? And how can one feel accomplishment in something never attained? One should set a destination that is within one's reach. As one reaches that point another slightly higher goal can be set—and so on, as one travels up the path. In this way the mountain can be climbed in increments. Look not at the vast mountain as a whole. Rather look minutely and scrutinize each individual step. There will thus be no discouragement, for every step is a success.

"A journey of ten thousand miles begins with each and every step."

SOLID CLIMBING

When climbing over steep terrain, one step must be placed lightly yet firmly before the other. A solid base is necessary from which one can build and progress. Nothing is more draining than to step forward only to feel one's support leg sliding back.

"Forward momentum needs something against which to push."

UNSTABLE TERRAIN

Some portion of every path is bound to be unstable. What looks firm and solid suddenly gives way underfoot. Thus, the climber must be wary of taking his terrain for granted. For, lulled into a false sense of security, many before him have fallen to their deaths. But don't take each step as a possible stride into the abyss. And don't take each step as though onto Cloud Nine into paradise. Simply take each step . . . for what it is.

RIDGELINES

The ridge often provides the best way to traverse. For loose rocks have been trampled upon. Rain and snow have weathered the uneven ground, filling in depressions, wearing away what protrudes.

In contrast, side-sloping (or walking the steep hillside) is an accident waiting to happen. Rocks are poised, and can't wait to tilt and fall.

The crest offers stability. The ridgeline is a secure avenue that should be followed whenever possible. The traveler remains high and balanced, gaining perspective and distance.

WHEN TO AVOID RIDGES

Lightning strikes whatever is on top. Cold winds buffet the unprotected ridge. In inclement weather, contouring or side-sloping offers shelter from the elements. To be near the top, but not on the top, is sometimes the safest approach. The experienced climber knows when and where to maintain a low profile.

FOLLOWING IN THE FOOTSTEPS

Whether traversing a snowfield or climbing an ice-covered ridge, "following-in-the-footsteps" conceals a double-edged sword. On the one hand, it conserves energy and staves off mental fatigue. Each step can be taken without bothering about placement. For someone else has already broken the trail.

On the other hand, trusting someone's footsteps may lead to disaster. For he may be lighter, more agile, or he may be totally inexperienced. Up ahead he may have taken a swan dive off a cliff.

Thus the veteran climber treats every footstep as his own. If it needs more depth, he digs his toes or heel. If the ice is melting or re-frozen, he simply chips a cleaner edge. He is conscious of every step whether or not it needs reworking. Unlike the novice, who is lulled into a daze, the true climber embraces each step, and each step is embraced by the mountain in return.

Mountain and climber are one. And, as one, there is nothing to fall.

DISPOSITION

Everyone knows that the journey is hard. Hence those of a cheerful, lighthearted disposition are invaluable along the more difficult passages. On the other hand, those of a sullen and despairing attitude make any situation that much more bleak. Many are the times that a slight joke or encouraging gesture was all that saved an expedition from certain failure. It provided the necessary impetus, the lifting of spirits, that made the difference between life and death.

ARROW POINT

In nature the most rapid group movement is accomplished by relegating the lead to a succession of high-paced members. A flock of birds, for example, will rotate the leader of the formation. The tip of the arrow flight-pattern works aerodynamically as a windbreak. He sets the faster pace and breaks the air for those who follow. Such a pace, however, cannot be sustained for long, and so the leader drops back as the next in line takes over. Thus the group moves at the fastest rate possible, not by the sustained efforts of one leader alone, but by a succession of leaders relieving each other of the burden of the task.

MOUNTAINS AND MOLEHILLS

Aspiration can turn a mountain into a molehill. Its lack can turn a molehill into a mountain. One must first decide what one really wants. Then strangely, all becomes quite simple. In fact nothing in the world can stand in the way. Like magic, the mountain becomes merely a molehill—the world is reduced to a grain of sand.

ISOLATION

The highest summit is the hardest to attain. The most difficult pass is the most dangerous. For this reason high-altitude climbers are necessarily the loneliest. One by one, fellow hikers are seduced by lower peaks until eventually one finds oneself traveling alone. More than frost or chilling winds, loneliness is the bitterest foe to those climbing the highest peak.

TRUE COLORS

In the Bowling Alley one's true color is shown. An avalanche of loose rocks sends the expedition scurrying for cover. Bruce is knocked off balance and is saved by Lee. I tumble out of control, and Tensing tackles me to the ground. Many leap for cover, while others jump into the turmoil to save the day. One member is free-falling while his "friend" jumps out of the way to save his own skin. Hamel, on the other hand, barges forth to soften the impact with his own body.

The aftermath is an eye-opener. Friendships are revaluated. True comrades come to light. Heroism and cowardice are unveiled in the blink of an eye.

Words and pretense are decoration. Reality is revealed with spontaneous action.

ROCKFALL

When scaling steep walls or gullies, care must be taken not to dislodge rocks and boulders on those below. The cautious climber must be ever aware of the underlying strata. For the pinnacle of achievement is nothing if it crushes those following your path.

DROP ZONE

The veteran climber is, conversely, also aware of the conditions above. For falling debris may, in turn, transform one into falling debris. Severe injury can be sustained in the wake of those who have gone before. At the very least, it can distract or turn one from the path.

Hence, it is best to always be higher than others. For then, if one comes to harm, the only climber to blame is oneself.

On the heights there is no fear of anything falling from above. And on the summit the only thing to fear falling is you.

SECOND WIND

At 22-27, after a preposterously slow start, the expedition experiences the fabled "second wind." Tensing has been prodding us to keep moving and get the lead out. We are at the point of exhaustion, but through insults and humiliation he rouses us from our torpor. Suddenly a weight is lifted from our shoulders. The struggle becomes a challenge, the game becomes easier. We double-time and sing cadence songs. We march and stride up the slope. Nothing can possibly stand in our way. For we have crossed a psycho-physical barrier.

One must attempt the impossible, push to the limit and then double it. Otherwise one remains forever in check. Strangely enough, by trying harder, things actually become easier. Whereas by moseying along, never pressing the task, that fine line, that octave jump, will never be crossed. "DRIVEN" is the word that characterizes the successful mountaineer.

CLIMBING THE MOUNTAIN

It takes everything I have to trudge up the steep slope. The brisk wind. The light snow. Panting, step by step, gasping for air. My thighs ache. Calf muscles strain. It is undoubtedly the most difficult task of my life. And yet strangely there is a liberating release, an incomparable clarity. Mind, body, spirit fuse into one.

Thoughts like snowflakes drift gently from the mind until eventually all have fallen. The mind has become clear. You and the mountain are all that remain. And finally—only the mountain.

THE MAD CLIMBERS

On K-7 we come upon the remnants of an earlier expedition. After struggling for hours up precipitous cracks and chimneys, we achieve the summit only to find two oddballs peering through sextants and telescopes. Bob and Dave they call themselves. They are charting and surveying while drinking Yeti beer and singing trail songs.

"Scoping out where you're going?" asks Adrian contemptuously. Adrian hated finding people where people shouldn't be.

Bob and Dave exchange conspiratorial glances and then break into jovial laughter. "More like trying to find out where we've been!"

To our surprise they claim to have climbed every Never Summer Mountain twice. And yet they are still no nearer to their goal—Pochen Point.

"Oh well," Dave says lightheartedly, "at least we know where not to go."

Bob chuckles nervously, almost crazily. "If only we knew where we were. Heck, when it comes right down to it, we might already be there."

There is a certain madness to climbing. At times one wakes up to find oneself hanging backwards off a cliff.

RE-UNION?

Still atop K-7, Tensing finally arrives to bring up the rear of the expedition.

"Hey!—Hey! Bob and Dave!—the Mad Mountaineers!" he laughs exuberantly.

"Tensing! You old Yeti. Haven't you had enough of the peaks?" asks Dave as the two embrace.

"Now my turn," says Tensing as Dave and Bob let each other go. Tensing and Dave embrace as Bob chuckles maniacally.

"Time to transcend," he teases, waving his finger in Tensing's face. Tensing and Bob then embrace. Then Tensing, Bob, and Dave embrace.

From a distance, the three together in their yak suits make a strange sight: a hulking hairy beast—suitable fodder for provoking legends.

COINCIDENCE

"Pochen Point?" queries Tensing with a mocking grin. "You're climbing Pochen Point?" he asks innocently with a lilt to his voice.

"Isn't everyone?" says Bob, glancing nervously askance.

"But weren't you looking for Pochen Point the last time we met?"

"Okay. Okay," Dave relents with embarrassment. "We've always been looking for Pochen Point. Can we join up with you or not?"

"Why not?" says Tensing. "The more the merrier."

"All right!" Bob shouts with glee. "Let's get going. Which way from here?"

Bob looks at Tensing. Tensing looks at Dave. Dave, Bob, and Tensing look at each other.

THE WAY DOWN

Bob, Dave, and Tensing peer over the summit of K-7.

"Oh no," laments Adrian. "You don't want us to go back down?"

"We just got here," I chime in. "What was the point?"

Adrian and I both look to Hamel for support. But the Barbarian just sits calmly with a grin.

"Well," says Tensing, "unless you have wings I propose the only possible choice. Shall we?" he gestures to Dave, extending his open hand invitingly over the abyss.

"No, no," Dave demurs, "after you."

"I'll go," says Bob. With telescope and sundry equipment on his back, Bob shouts "Geronimo!", leaps off and goes sliding down the scree chute. Dave follows close behind. The two hoot and holler, laughing madly as they slip and careen over the steep talus slope.

"They say we are mad. But really we are not quite mad enough."

BOULDER HOPPING

The Sound of One Foot Falling

"Let yourself go," says Tensing as I kneel, adjusting and re-tying my boots. My feet ache from the constant downward jamming and pressure. "You're holding yourself back. You must learn to flow down the mountain allowing gravity to do the work. Let your body glide naturally from rock to rock. Let go of the fear that pulls you back."

"But if I trip, if I fall . . ."

"Only one foot can be tripped at a time."

BEARINGS

At the bottom of the couloir Dave and Bob are once again taking readings. Bob seems disturbed, gyrating while peering down at his compass.

"I can never get these dang things to work. It keeps pointing in different directions."

Adrian smiles smugly as he examines the shiny black boulders along the slope.

"Magnetite!" he exclaims in triumph. "You won't get accurate readings around here."

"It doesn't matter," says Dave. "We don't know where to go anyway."

Tensing arrives and unravels the tattered scroll of our journey. The ancient map falls to pieces, but he is seemingly unconcerned. Instead, he and Dave busily determine our course from the remaining fragments.

"Mount Skull," says Dave with finality.

"Sounds good to me," says Tensing, "if the ridge isn't too difficult for these novices. It would sure save time. We might even get down before dark."

We all look across to the ominous shadows of Mount Skull—its hollow darkness deepening with the dropping angle of the setting sun. It would be a veritable race with light.

THE KNIFE EDGE

The knife edge gleams. Golden sunlight glances off the serrated ridge, dancing and sparkling in the glow of the setting sun. We were counting on the northern face of Mount Skull as a faster descent route. But one look at the jutting pinnacles sends chills down my spine. For once I can appreciate the adage "living on the edge." Its imagery is borne out in the sleek, black rain-polished granite. One slip means disaster. Balance honed to an art is a necessary adjunct to life on the edge. It is a tentative delicacy, a thrilling moment by moment expectation. We stand in awed silence—reverence for the challenge, the impossibility. But for now the sheen of the knife edge will be saved for another time. The expedition will descend through the gentle, yellow-orange alpenglow of the west ridge.

LETTING GO

It isn't long before Bob, Dave, Hamel, and Adrian are out of sight. Like antelopes or mountain goats they bound gracefully away without cares. The rest of the expedition drags wearily behind—stepping timidly, fearfully over each and every rock.

Tensing brings up the rear, herding the stragglers together.

"You guys sure are slow," he laughs, jokingly serious. "Your fear is exhausting you, holding you back, countering your gravity. You must let go, enter the flow, feel the exhilarating lightness of the descent. Become one with the mountain slope, align yourself with its angular pull. It is your ally for a quick descent, not an obstacle for your fear."

"Watch me," he says cheerfully. And in a moment he vanishes into the dusk.

It is sometimes easier and more graceful
to keep the momentum going,
than it is to apply the brakes and rest.

NIGHT-FALL

With the last glint of light over the Never Summer Mountains we are engulfed by darkness. It isn't long before even the vague outlines of boulders are lost. We try following Tensing's advice, but without light we are soon tripping over projecting rocks, turning our feet in invisible crevices. The expedition is reduced to a bumbling troupe of clowns, a traveling circus of buffoonery. We collide with each other, carom off rocks, stumble and are sent sprawling. Grunts of pain and cursing are our only link in the void.

Without warning, dark figures suddenly loom before us. Five black shapes silhouetted menacingly against the night. The expedition barely avoids a collision before pulling back with a start. It is Tensing and his cohorts. They had been standing vigil, silently awaiting our arrival like unmoving monoliths—empowered guardians of the night.

NIGHT-WALKING

Tensing says we are klutzes.

"If Hamel, with his bulk, can gracefully night-walk, then so can all of you."

The Barbarian then proceeds to teach the "Sherpa Art" of night-walking. First he calls for silence.

"No fidgeting. No movement."

A gentle breeze rustles the tundra grass. Some of us begin to sway and totter.

"You're too high and top-heavy," Hamel admonishes. "Drop lower, find your still-point, your center of balance. Keep your back erect, gaze forward, knees bent slightly like you're just beginning to sit down in a chair."

We assume the position and are motionless in the night.

"Feel the earth beneath your feet. Imagine an expanding cushion connecting them to the ground. Your knees are springy shock absorbers that can adjust to any bump."

As we ready ourselves for the descent, Hamel makes one more remark.

"Feel the night, the earth, the breeze as you glide past. Move with your center, not with your head."

GROUNDING

It is astonishing how efficiently a spirited teacher can impart knowledge. Within an hour of infrequent stumbles, the expedition is gliding swiftly through the dark. It is a challenge, a rush, a carefree flow with the night. Even somber Adrian's enthusiasm seems to be labeling it "fun."

Tensing considers making a high-altitude camp, but with novices along he elects dropping below timberline.

"Besides, they need as much night-walking practice as they can get. They'll need it when we climb S-2 in the dark."

A true climber knows all aspects of his mountain. He can climb in any weather, under any condition, night or day.

NIGHT 14

Camp is set up with little difficulty in the dark—a fringe benefit of our communion with the night. Tents are propped, bags unrolled, fires built (good thing we dropped to timberline where there is wood). All of us are exhausted yet exuberant over our success. An openness and camaraderie fill the evening air. During the clear, star-lit supper, Bob and Dave chide Tensing.

"So," says Bob innocently while grinning like a Cheshire Cat, "is it true what they say?"

"How does it feel?" Dave says teasingly. "Do you feel like a real Sherpa?—a Sherpa of the Black Sash."

"Speech!" cry Bruce and Lee.

"Give us a speech!" "A profound speech!" sing out others from around the campfire.

PROCESS

Tensing's Saga Continues

Tensing clears his voice. A sudden chill pervades the air.

"I have been granted the Sherpa level of the Black Sash, but what does it mean? The strange thing is that I still feel like a beginner. The more I learn, the more I see there is to learn—so much that I don't know. There is no end in sight." Tensing pauses and gazes off into the dark, pinnacled horizon.

"Perhaps it is a process. Or perhaps the end, the goal, is the process. It reminds me of the saying that it is not the goal that matters, but simply the path. And then some say that what matters is not even the path, but rather the passage—the pathless path."

"Bravo!" we all cheer and applaud. Tensing makes his bows. And then one by one we turn in and fall asleep.

DAY 15

We awaken to a warm, morning breeze. It is amazing how dropping a few thousand feet can make such a dramatic difference in weather.

Hamel says that he has been atop peaks in freezing blizzards only to descend and, within an hour, be sweltering under a summer sun. Adrian says it's why he enjoys alpine hiking.

"You can observe so many diverse ecosystems. Plants and animals that exist at the top of the world can be seen with only a one-mile climb. The climatic zones of a high peak parallel the zones between the equator and the poles. The mountain is a virtual microcosm of the entire planet. As one climbs a mountain, one is climbing the world."

UNREST

There is brief unrest as Tensing surveys our course. He is looking down into the canyons and valleys.

"Oh no," says Adrian. "You don't want us to go down there?"

"We just got here," I chime in. "What was the point?"

Adrian and I both look to Hamel for support. But the Barbarian just sits calmly with a grin.

"Well," Tensing says to Adrian, "you just said you enjoyed the full range of ecosystems. And there they are," he remarks with a downward sweep of the hand. "The valleys and deserts are waiting below."

"But we're supposed to be climbing!" snaps Adrian. "What's the point of going up and down? Up and down!"

Tensing looks behind at the vast Never Summer Mountains. His arms and hands splay outward in a gesture of mock helplessness.

"But I don't see Pochen Point here—do you?"

Adrian is contrite. He looks down and plays with his gauntlets in embarrassment, toying with the idea of throwing one down.

"Pochen Point is over there!" Tensing announces assuredly. "Across the canyons and desert floor into the next range of mountains—the Borgonian Mountains."

A shudder passes through the expedition. Even the Barbarian grimaces and turns away. However Bob and Dave, the Mad Climbers, seem totally delighted.

"So that's why we never found it," Bob says, stupefied. "We were climbing in the wrong place!"

THE DREADED BORGONIAN MOUNTAINS

71

ADAPTABLE

The most adept traveler knows when to alter course. Plans are never written in stone. Chance encounters, sudden disasters, changes in weather—should all lead one to revaluate the path.

While persistence is often a virtue, a simple-minded stubbornness can be a bane. The astute hiker will merely by-pass a fallen tree, rather than moving or chopping it away.

THE RIGHT PLACE

"The right place is over there—somewhere," says Tensing with a hearty laugh. "I'm almost sure of it," he adds with a grin.

All of us are frightened and depressed. It means dropping to the valley floor and starting all over. All the elevation we had struggled for would be lost.

"That's life," says Tensing cheerfully. "Sometimes it's up. Sometimes it's down. As my Head Sherpa used to say, 'Get knocked down seven times, get up eight!' "

"Now wait a second," objects Adrian. "That's not logical. How can you get up more times than you've been down?"

UP AND DOWN

Along any path there are sure to be ups and downs. Peaks and valleys are natural to most terrains. For this reason one should learn the art of downward climbing as a complement to that of upward climbing. The essence of the downward climb is contained in one principle: Momentum. With any descent, momentum and acceleration should be generated so as to travel more easily up the next slope. If one moves slowly downward, one will move even more slowly upward.

The path is a mirror, the way one falls reflecting the way one rises. The true tests of life concern not the ups, but the downs. For dealing with adversity develops character and soul.

RESTING ON THE UPHILL

When given the option, never rest at the base of a hill. In such undulating terrain, with many ups and downs, always reach a crest before stopping to rest. The physical and psychological ease of starting level, or downhill, contrasts with the pain and dismay of having to start up on the incline. In fact, after cresting, one may no longer need a break, for continuing flat or downhill is, itself, a rest.

THE UNKNOWN

Tensing searches for the tattered scroll of our journey and it is found to be missing—literally! It has disintegrated through wear, and all that remains is the one fragment showing Pochen Point. But without relation to anything else it is seemingly useless. Tensing keeps it anyway, perhaps as a memento of our journey.

The Mad Climbers' maps and charts are also useless, for they were only of the Never Summer Mountain Range. "We didn't know it was a Borgonian Mountain," they claim by way of excuse.

"Well then," Tensing says decisively, "we must create our own map."

RESPONSIBILITY

It is decided that the expedition will separate to scope out and chart the unknown terrain. We will branch out to points overlooking the desert valley, and then rendezvous at the confluence of this canyon's creek with the valley river.

Bob and Dave, knowing their instruments, will attempt to map possible ascent routes into the Borgonian Mountains. Tensing will travel alone for reasons he will not disclose. Adrian, Bruce and Lee will reconnoiter the left flank, while Hamel will take three members to the right. These two groups will chart a course through the desert valley to the base of the Borgonian Range. Then, horror upon horrors, Tensing wants me to lead the remaining two members down the creek to the Confluence and search for a place to ford.

"But I can't do that!" I object. "I'm just a novice like all the rest!"

But Tensing is adamant. "There is no one else. Besides," he assures confidently, "how can you possibly get lost?"

HONOR IS SECRET

We are preparing for the descent, splitting up rations and supplies for what is anticipated to be a one week separation. In my case an ordeal. I can't believe what's happening. I don't know anything about mountain-climbing. I wouldn't know how to respond in an emergency.

When no one is looking, Tensing saunters over and ties a black sash around my left upper arm.

"Quickly, put on your coat before someone sees."

"But what's this for?" I ask as I slip on my coat. I am baffled, and yet I am bursting with pride.

"Don't tell anybody," Tensing says in mock complicity.

BLACK SASH WITH SHERPA
BADGE OF HONOR

NO DISTINCTION

Although I achieve the black sash, Tensing warns me of its emptiness.

"What difference does a piece of cloth make?" he asks. "You are still you. I am still me. What does it matter the color or degree? You are at level one. I am at level six. The Head Sherpa is at level nine. The others are all the colors of the rainbow underneath. But what difference does it make? There are the five white sashes of beginning innocence, then seven colors of the rainbow, then ten levels of black. But then what?" he pauses. "Level ten of black is the highest one can achieve while alive. Eleven and twelve can only be bestowed after one's death. And do you know what color they are?" Tensing pauses again while I ponder the answer. "Eleven and twelve are once again the color white! The highest point one can reach is the level at which one began. White—the beginning and the end—there is no distinction."

LOSING THE WAY

The dense undergrowth is undoubtedly the cause of our losing the path. Small game trails and sidetracks branch so deceptively and so unnoticeably that we soon find the trail petering off into underbrush or over an outcrop of rocks. Tensing warned me not to panic should this happen.

"The path," he explained, "must be lost in order to be found. It is natural that one should lose one's way. For, after all, is not what we search for the pathless path? Is not the movement in itself truly the way?"

CHOICES

"But whichever way I go seems to be the wrong choice," I complain to Tensing in my dreams.

He merely smiles enigmatically.

"There are no wrong choices along the way. There are only choices. There is only the way."

RECONNAISSANCE

The Forest for the Trees

Tensing had once explained that when lost, the best tactic is to gain the high ground. Search for the closest ridge, peak, or even the tallest tree. One must rise above the surroundings in order to determine one's position. One must distance oneself in order to gain perspective. Hikers call this tactic "gaining the high ground." Folk wisdom calls it "not seeing the forest for the trees."

Climbers must therefore be the least lost of all. For the higher one goes, the more apparent is the way. And from the highest point in the world everything else can be clearly seen.

OFF THE BEATEN TRACK

Upon the Lower Point Crags we come upon evidence of a Yeti lookout. We are frightened and yet in awe as we gaze at the tools and instruments that no man has ever seen. No human has walked this way before.

Only by clearing your own path can something new be discovered. The tracks of others may be easier to follow, but this is because so many have been there before. To make the unusual find, to see the unique vista, is possible only for those who chance the unknown.

CHALLENGES

Only with new challenges are the climber's skills enhanced. By always taking the easiest path nothing worthwhile is attained. To become a superior climber one must face the unknown, the unexpected. One must attempt more difficult routes, learn new strategies and better holds. One must do what is harder, what is more dangerous.

It often seems easiest to pursue the present course. It feels safe and secure simply to slug it up the gradual incline. For a fall would be a mere stumble, at most an inconsequential bruise.

It takes courage and faith to suddenly spring onto the cliff-face—to make the quantum leap that can lead to disaster or death. The truth be known: no climber to achieve stature could be called faint-hearted. Each has surmounted the inner obstacles, overcome the trepidation in his heart.

KNOWING WHEN TO ADVANCE

Along the path lies a fine line between boldness and foolhardiness. If one is timid one may as well stay at home, safe and sound. Risk is necessary in revealing new vistas and exploring new terrain.

And yet, daring and courage can be tantamount to recklessness if the risk far outweighs any possible gain. For what's the point of seeking challenges if one loses everything along the way?

The most successful adventurer thus strikes a balance between staying and moving forward. He knows when to say "yes," and when to say "no."

BUSHWHACKING

Despite Tensing's assurances that we can't possibly get lost, we find ourselves lost somewhere near the Confluence. As leader I remain calm and seemingly cheerful, but the others are doubtful. For we are trapped within a maze of meandering and branching canyons. And chance is our only possible rendezvous and escape.

The path before us is choked with weeds and tangled bushes. What's worse, we don't even know if it's the right one. We push through all the same, forcing our way, scratching and cutting our arms and legs. High ground game trails along the upper bank. Then dropping down for a rocky then muddy stretch along the dry, stream bed. Then up again and down again, backtracking and bushwhacking. The procedure is exhausting. It takes three times longer to travel without a path. And not only does it take longer, but it's mentally fatiguing. For one must sense at every turn the way one should proceed. Each moment is a conscious choice. Which way is best? Through the trees and undergrowth, down along the bank, up along the rocky ledge, to the right or left into adjoining canyons?

What haunts us is not knowing whether we've passed the Confluence. Each step forward may be taking us one step farther from our goal. Instead of making time we may be losing it twice over. This lingering feeling that we may need to backtrack makes forward progress tentative. We lack confidence and thus can engage no commitment.

FINDING ONE'S WAY

Determining the correct course is half the battle. Regardless of difficulty, knowing which way to go makes progress a snap.

Being lost or uncertain drains energy and morale. Movement is fatiguing since it may all be for nothing.

The true path, once determined, acts as a beacon or magnet. One's will and energy merely pull one along the way.

RENDEZVOUS

DAY 23

We rendezvous with the others, but the expedition is itself lost.

"This won't do," says Tensing as he examines Adrian's map. "It's not big enough. It doesn't show enough detail. Where's the Lower Crags? How will we know where the Yeti are?"

"But Tensing," Adrian pleads, "we couldn't fit it on the map. Maybe if it were three times bigger we'd have space for the Yeti, but we didn't have the paper. We couldn't include everything. That's not logical. There just wasn't enough room."

"Not logical my foot," cries Tensing, stomping his boot.

Hamel and his group just now arrive. One of the haggard members stumbles over a jutting rock.

"You see!" exclaims Tensing triumphantly. "That rock isn't even on the map."

THE BEST MAP

Tensing looks at everyone's charts while shaking his head in dismay. "No precision. No accuracy. There is no detail."

"Well, what do you expect?" asks Adrian in disgust. "A map five times bigger?"

"That would be better," replies Tensing.

"Ten times bigger?"

"Even better."

"Twenty times?"

"Better still. The bigger, the better," says Tensing with a crazed glare in his eyes. "Eventually, as the Head Sherpa once said, the best map would be a one-to-one correspondence with reality. Such a map, when unfolded, would cover the entire world. Anything less is just not quite right." Tensing tears up our maps before our eyes—the maps we had spent an entire week painstakingly charting.

"Gentlemen," announces Tensing with a grandiose spreading of his arms. "Let me introduce you to the perfect map—that of the world."

A ONE-TO-ONE CORRESPONDENCE

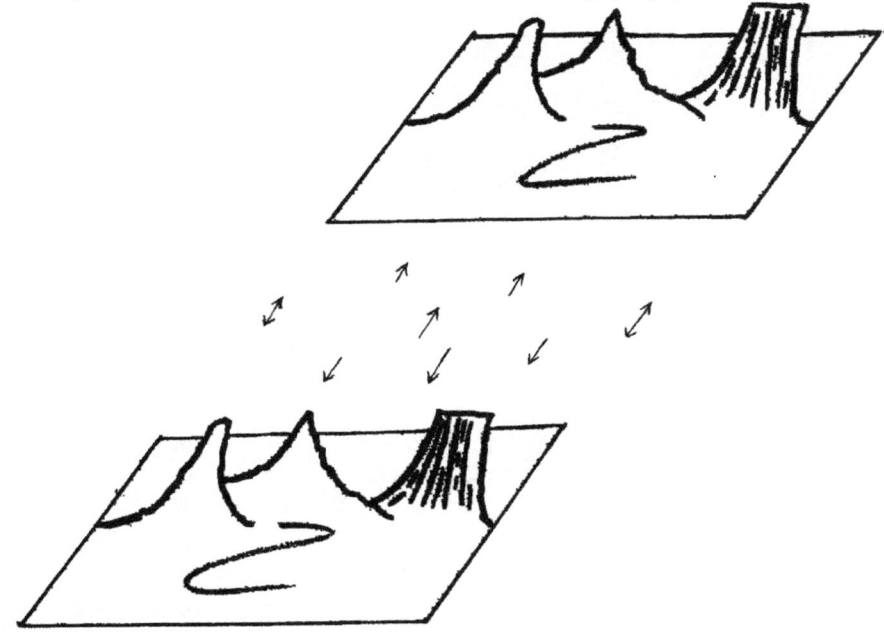

THE NON-FORD

"I hope it wasn't too difficult," Tensing quizzes me with a sly grin. "You didn't get lost did you?"

"No way," I say. Now that the ordeal is over I am embarrassed by all my complaining and lack of fortitude. "It was a piece of cake," I maintain with confidence.

"Well then," says Tensing seriously, "where are we to ford?"

The expedition breaks up laughing. The Barbarian rolls uncontrollably on the ground. Dave and Bob hug each other with mirth. The joke is on us all, me particularly, for the Confluence no longer exists. In this dry climate, streams and rivers flow only after periodic cloudbursts. Within a day or two all water drains off or soaks into the ground. My assigned task was really no task at all. The Confluence was only an illusion in my mind.

THE DREADED NON-FORD

100

OBSTACLES OF MIND

When to Cross the Bridge

The greatest obstacles along the way exist only in the mind. More energy is spent worrying and procrastinating than is ever spent on the situation itself. Freeing the mind of imaginary obstacles conserves vital energy. And thus, confronting the real obstacle (if it is ever even encountered) usually presents far less difficulty than originally assumed.

"Step forward with your foot, not with your mind."

IMPASSE

After all the obstacles skirted, the trouble and disasters overcome, the worst disruption to the expedition comes in a seemingly innocuous form. It is Day 27 when we encamp at Peekaboo Crossroads near the "ford." Lobsam, a delightful tot from a nearby village, adopts our camp as his personal playground. He is everywhere, keeping us company, doing small chores, and playing games. At lunch he stands motionless gazing up at a mushrooming cloud.

"What keeps clouds in the air?" he asks Adrian who, for the first time, is nonplussed. There are no reins to Lobsam's curiosity and that is our downfall.

Early the next morning we awaken to the sound of Lobsam's giggle. He arrives to stake first claim on the new day. But the expedition is breaking camp and so we must say our good-byes.

"But where are you going?" he asks heartbroken. We tell him "Pochen Point" and he just sighs.

"But you just got here," he insists. "Why do you have to go?"

WHY?

Through that one three-letter word the expedition suffers its greatest loss. We leave Peekaboo all right, but the difficulties that were formerly taken for granted soon become an overwhelming burden. Efficiency and discipline deteriorate. Members wander off and are long in returning. Even the best and strongest become listless and despondent. Adrian quips that it is all Lobsam's fault. But Tensing says that we should have known "Why?" from the start.

"Too often people merely drift along with others, never forging a self-determined path."

DAY 39

What, indeed, am I doing in this godforsaken landscape? Why am I here? What am I proving? A sudden afternoon downpour has caught us unprepared, and so we huddle beneath a hulking column of sandstone. We are muddy and miserable, drenched and shivering as the wind lashes through us to the small, smoldering fire.

Here I am on an expedition that is sapping my life's energy. Here I am trying to climb an unscalable peak—a trek that could very well be fatal. And for what? What could be worth the risk and suffering? To climb a legendary mountain that might not even exist?—a hidden mountain rumored to be the world's tallest. And even if it does exist, even if it is the tallest, even if we do reach the top. What then? Where do we go from there? Was this to be my life's sole purpose?

DAY 47

In a dream at Nymph Spring I come to terms with my gadfly. Tensing has been talking in soft undertones over a crackling fire. We sit mesmerized by the glowing embers and the flickering flames. The radiant heat makes my eyes heavy, my mind drowsy and delirious. It seems that I have been listening for hours. Tensing alone drones on as I fall half-asleep, and suddenly all my troubles vanish. With childish exuberance I feel at home with my companions. I realize that I will always be on this journey. Imagining myself elsewhere is too alien, too much a dream. For the first time Tensing commends my insight.

"'Why?' is a delusion. When you can imagine no alternative then you are certainly upon the path."

NO TURNING BACK

At noon on Day 54 Tensing holds a conference to determine our fate.

"Gentlemen," he says in mock solemnity, "today is the day. You must decide now and for the rest of your life."

A chilling wind howls through the canyon. A bleak overcast and circling ravens make the melodrama complete. Adrian produces a list of specifics. He begins to read off an inventory of supplies. But Tensing waves him off.

"We are midway to Pochen Point. We have consumed half our rations. Winter is approaching and time is growing short. You must turn back now or continue all the way. One or the other. And the choice must be now. There will be no mediocre efforts or you will surely die. If you continue, you must continue all the way or you will die. Beyond this point you will lack sufficient provisions for the return. All or nothing. There is no middle-ground.

ALL OR NOTHING

Within the confines of Box Canyon the expedition sits in conference. After an hour of heated controversy three members opt for the return. It was more than they expected. More they could not bear.

Tensing adds further to our consternation by noting that the journey thus far has been mere child's play.

"You must be prepared to sacrifice totally, risk everything. For holding back, the slightest reluctance, will spell disaster. From here the path grows ever more hazardous. Most of you will never even see the top. And none of you should expect to return."

After further reflection, two more members nonchalantly choose to turn back, making five in all. Excluding Tensing, the remaining expedition now comprises seven.

BREAKUP

Provisions have been split for those who will return. It is considered to be a parting of ways. There is sadness and reluctance, frustrating self-doubts and second thoughts. But in the end it has already been decided. The return party departs carrying messages to the lowlands. Strangely, not one turns for a final gesture of farewell. They have already left the expedition.

"Well now," says Tensing with relief, "things will go much easier."

"Easier!" exclaims Adrian. "You just said it would be harder!"

"It would have been harder—for them." Adrian looks befuddled and so Tensing resumes. "But you see, unless you are willing to commit fully, sacrifice and let go, every step forward will be dragging you down. You must first release your grasp in order to flow upward to the top."

DEPARTURES

I can't believe it. How could this be happening? How could people be together for so long, share experiences and mutual growth, and then separate—forever.

"That's life," remarks Tensing.

But it was impossible to accept. How could people enter your life, share a common bond, a trust, and then leave—just like that? Tears well up as I watch the departing members fade into the distance—tiny black figures merging into the landscape. The challenges and fun times, the hardship and childish banter, the camaraderie and horseplay would be no more.

"Look at it this way," says Tensing cheerfully as solace, "in life, just as on a journey, people meet and intermingle and then go their separate ways. Most people are merely tourists whose intimacy should be taken lightly, for no matter how sincere, a tourist must eventually return home. True fellow travelers, comrades for life, are really quite rare, almost extinct—although others are often mistaken for them in the wild. This rare breed is hard to distinguish, but once identified they should be cherished and readily embraced.

A NEW BEGINNING

We can start fresh from Day One. The expedition has a new beginning. Tensing explains that one's fellow travelers can either help or hinder one along the way. For that reason discrimination in choice is essential. At any moment one should be ready to depart. At any moment one should be ready to greet others with open arms.

The problem with most travelers is that they never really choose their partners. They allow themselves to drift along like so much flotsam or debris, picking up whatever sticks and accumulates by chance or whim.

"No wonder they never get anywhere!" Tensing says with disgust.

DAY 57

Tensing explains that, despite our loss of elevation, we are nevertheless making progress.

"This desert may look low, but it's actually a high-altitude plateau. Even with our loss in elevation, we are still over two miles higher than when we began."

The expedition is incredulous. Bob and Dave break out their instruments and begin taking readings.

"It is an illusion," assures Tensing. "It only seems like we're low."

"But we haven't been climbing!" argues Adrian in disbelief.

"Gradually, imperceptibly, ever since the Non-Ford. You're just in better condition. You didn't notice the strain."

"But we keep getting lost," I object. "How can we be getting anywhere?"

Tensing laughingly explains that it's a natural part of the terrain.

"Meandering, rambling around—in these twisted gorges and canyons—it's the only way to go about!"

CONTINENTAL DRIFT

"And what's more," explains Tensing, "there is a subtle factor to contend with . . . Among veteran climbers the phenomenon is known as 'flexible mountains.' It is a hidden, discreet process, but it is happening all the time."

Adrian waves his hand excitedly like a schoolboy and chimes in. "I know what you're talking about. Modern science refers to the process as 'continental drift.' Formerly a theory, it has now been proven as fact. It is responsible for altering the face of the world, and it is happening indiscernibly at this very moment."

"And so objective research confirms," says Tensing in a somber tone. "The mountains are folding, compressing, undulating, in constant flux. They are not the unmoving monoliths they show themselves to be in the light of day. For, overnight, when no one's looking, their positions can change."

The expedition gasps in disbelief. The only stability in our lives has suddenly been torn from under our feet.

"With patience," admits Tensing, "even Bob and Dave's crude instruments could catch the changes in the act." Tensing goes on to explain that this is the reason we so often find ourselves lost. For the landscape is continuously changing. From moment to moment the terrain is never the same.

"Haven't you ever scaled the wrong ridge, ascended a false peak? Weren't you certain when you began, that your orientation was correct? What had happened in the meantime? The answer is simple: continental drift. The mountains had flexed their muscles overnight. What was once the highest peak suddenly slumps from sight. Entire ridges buckle out of nowhere and separate you from your goal. What was once so close, becomes so far . . ."

All members of the expedition nod their heads in wonder. It explained so many of their past mistakes.

THE FLEXIBLE MOUNTAINS

(REVISED)

Bruce and Lee are in jovial fits of laughter

"So that's what you meant," Bruce chortles at Lee. "You knew it all the time!" The rest of the expedition wants in on the joke.

"I never understood," explains Bruce. "But as each climbing season began, like clockwork, my friend Lee would lose all interest in the world. He would become obsessed with taking every opportunity to climb. Nothing else really seemed to matter. And the excuse he gave was always a puzzle."

"The world," states Lee matter-of-factly on cue, "will always be here. But the mountains can change at any time."

"And besides," continues Lee, "what's more important? Your job, your life, a meaningful relationship?—or going off by yourself and scaling a mountain? The answer is simple: climbing a mountain all alone. For the world is here and now, whereas mountains are transcendent."

DEAD? ENDS

Trapped in a labyrinth of dead-end canyons the expedition succumbs to hopelessness and frustration. But Hamel remains as cheerful as ever. While Tensing seems positively exuberant.

"We're on the verge," encourages Hamel.

"We're coming ever closer," chimes in Tensing.

Adrian is perplexed while I am as dumbfounded as ever. But Sherpa psychology has a logic of its own.

Dead ends are not a waste of time and energy, for one has gained a valuable lesson where not to go.

Eliminate the dead ends and one finds oneself closer to the true path.

RE-COGNITION

Looking back has its purpose: remembering where you are. "You are here," is mapped indelibly onto the brain. If one is led into a blind alley, one can quickly backtrack and start over. For not every possible path will lead to the goal. In fact, most paths meander and can lead one astray. Therefore, by remembering a cliff-face, a boulder, the cut up a gully—one can hastily retreat and keep from becoming lost.

It is the amateur hiker who wanders in circles, for to him everything looks the same. With experience, the savvy traveler recognizes the landscape. Deep within, he has a sense of where he is, and from where he came.

ENCIRCLEMENT

The expedition spends nine days meandering in a circle within a labyrinth of twisted gorges and game trails. We realize it as we stumble onto one of our previous camps. The members of the expedition are tired and discouraged, but according to Tensing our way would soon be made clear. We encamp in our old spots and with a feeling of déjà vu we retire.

At sunrise, before we can forget, Tensing has us relate our dreams. Though some are vague and seemingly irrelevant, our leader is able to map our coordinates, pieced together from the fragments of our dreams. From this psycho-geographical data he successfully plots our escape from the maze.

DREAM MAPPING

MY VISION OF
THE SPECTACLE

HAMEL'S YETI
SIGNAL OUTPOST

LOWER POINT CRAGS

DAVE'S ENCOUNTER
WITH MOTHER
PTARMIGAN

K-7

ADRIAN'S ENTRAPMENT IN
RARE BORGONITE CRYSTAL FOREST

REARWARD ASSAULTS

We cross Desolation Plateau at an altitude of 12,094 feet on Day 66. The gale-force wind thrashes us as we traverse the open plateau. Hats are stripped off our heads, gloves torn from our hands and sent sailing over the cliff. Not only is the wind in our face, making forward progress next to impossible, but every step is accompanied by a gasping effort to breathe. The constant blast of air into my nose and mouth makes me choke and turn away. On turning back I catch sight of Tensing up ahead. His cheery face and laughing eyes are a mockery of my struggle. He waves his arms gaily as he presses backward into the invisible wall of wind. I follow suit, as do the others, and with amazement find moving and breathing easier.

"You see," Tensing later explains, "progress may sometimes be the opposite of what it seems. Occasionally one must appear to be going down when in reality one is going up."

FEAR

DAY 67

We arrive at the foothills of the Borgonian Mountains. Despite halfhearted attempts at bravado, the expedition is still wary of traveling into this range. All remember the harrowing legends of Borgonian spirits and monsters from childhood. Death. Madness. Suicide and murder.

"Forget those childish fears," says Tensing. "For by far, the worst thing you will ever encounter is your own self. Once you confront your self everything else becomes child's play."

DAY 69

AND TREMBLING

We hear a few shrieks echoing through the canyons.

"Banshee cries, just fallen timber scraping against a standing tree," explains Tensing.

See a few looming shadows around dusk.

"Yeti, just Yeti, nothing to worry about," Tensing assures.

Smell roasting flesh.

"Hallucinations. Wishful thinking. Yeti and Sherpas are vegetarian. You're the ones I'm worried about."

Feel an ominous presence as we are suddenly shaken from behind.

"Hey, hey! Just joking," laughs Hamel. "Just trying to keep you on your toes."

NIGHT 70

While camped at Isolation Lake even Hamel shakes with fear.

"It's just the cold wind," he tries covering himself. "Maybe it's hypothermia," he grins hopefully.

Out of the corner of my eye I catch two indistinct shapes loping into the dark.

"Look at it this way," says Tensing, trying to console us. "You've got nothing to lose. What can possibly happen? Madness? Most of you are half-mad anyway."

Bob and Dave eye each other furtively and sidle apart.

"Suicide? You've already killed yourself by joining the expedition. How can you kill yourself any more?"

"Murder? If what's out there doesn't get you, I certainly will—that is, if you don't do what I say and forget your superstitions. You'll have enough just handling the natural terrain. Don't try surmounting the supernatural terrain as well."

FRENZY

Despite Tensing's admonitions the expedition is in a frenzy. The Mad Climbers stomp their feet while pulling and tearing at their hair.

"An ancient Sherpa practice to conquer fear," Tensing comments offhandedly.

Bruce and Lee go crazy, punching and kicking at each other, leaping and spinning through the air. I try to stop them, to break up the fight, but Tensing intercedes.

"They are doing double kata," he explains. But his words mean nothing. I remain bewildered. "Tibetan kung-fu," he adds. "Ritualized combat forms. It helps them center, distracts them from their fear, generates courage and energy. Prepares them for battle."

"Battle against what?" I asked perplexed.

But we are interrupted by Adrian who paces back and forth, rambling and muttering to himself. "I must remain calm. There is nothing to fear. Even if there is something to fear, worrying won't help at all."

Suddenly an eerie wail penetrates the night. My hair stands on end. Everyone stops and looks up at Hamel who is perched on a nearby pinnacle howling at the moon. It is a strange, half-groaning guttural cry—an alien song bemoaning a tragic loss.

EAVESDROPPING

"It's all right," says Tensing in a soft, comforting tone.

It is the dead of night and all other members are asleep. I awaken to the sound of quiet words. Motionless, I listen to Tensing's voice, but I have no idea with whom he is speaking.

"Don't worry," he says, "they're not coming for you. It's too late. You've made the choice. There's nothing more they can do."

Silence. Stillness. The crackling of the fire.

"Just remember who you are. That's all it takes. Remember who you are. By being yourself you can never falter or misstep. For being a myth is easy. Being real is hard."

REMEMBERING

"I remember a strange dream," Adrian says in astonishment the next morning. "And that's odd, because I usually never dream. I'm just not the type."

"Oh boy, Alcheringa dream-time," says Bob while gobbling down his breakfast of yak cheese and Sherpa gorp.

With great effort, Adrian places both palms against his head and recalls his dream.

"I dreamt I was on a strange, magical expedition. We were climbing the highest mountain in the world—a legendary mountain in a far-off land. The problem is that I woke up and found myself here."

Adrian pauses in consternation.

"Now I don't know whether I am really on an expedition relating a dream of an expedition, or whether I am dreaming I am on an expedition relating a dream of an expedition—and, if so, where am I now?"

"Oh boy," Bob sighs in exasperation.

USING YOUR HEAD

"I think Adrian is going bonkers," Bob whispers to me and Dave. "I think he thinks too much."

"It's rumored that high altitudes can affect mental functions," says Dave gravely, "but I don't know if I really believe it. Why, look at you and me. We've been mountain-climbing all our lives!"

Bob looks at Dave. Dave looks at Bob. Bob and Dave look askance.

"Well then, how else do you explain that dream?" asks Bob.

Dave and I look at each other and then look at Bob. We are silently rapt in thought.

"I have dreams like that all the time. In fact, I think I'm having one right now."

We all look at each other, puzzled. No one has said a word. Slowly, uncomfortably, we get up and leave.

"I" HAVE A DREAM

That night, at 26-34, I encounter the EGO-maniac! It is a blustering, big-headed, many-feathered fiend. He appears as one of us, although I can't quite say whom. Tensing soothes the precocious beast by promising to perform his one-legged dance. He then riddles it with a Sherpa koan: "What is the sound of one foot thumping?"

The EGO is momentarily stupefied, but only momentarily. Bob, Dave, and Hamel then intercede with a coordinated distraction. The Mad Climbers entertain by chanting trail-songs, while Hamel wails accompanying lullabies to the night.

Hamel: "Ho-hum. Ho-hum.

The day is done.

The night has come."

Refrain:

Bob: "I'm not me."

Dave (pointing at Bob): "He's not he."

Bob and Dave together: "None of us are sure we're we."

The fragile EGO bursts asunder out of hilarious sobs of oneness.

DAY 72

A lingering strangeness and tentative panic permeates the expedition. In order to alleviate our fears, Tensing employs the Sherpa psychology of distraction. Having taught us the Sherpa art of centering on the down-climb we are now to learn the art of serenity.

"Serenity is the quality of calmness and quiet."

Bob sits nodding his head in anxious agreement, thumping his foot nervously up and down like a neurotic rabbit.

"Calmness," says Tensing, "often means being still."

Bob stops thumping. All others freeze self-consciously.

"Relaxed stillness," resumes Tensing. The expedition releases its tension with a sigh.

"The Master of Serenity just happens to be with us here today. Perhaps he will deign to bestow upon us a few words."

"Me!" I yell, incredulous, totally distraught.

SHOW-TIME

"Here! Here!" cry my fellow travelers. "Give us a speech! A good speech! A story! A dream!"

"How is it you remain calm while others verge on panic?" asks Tensing. He sits contentedly, hands enfolded over his portly belly, smiling like a sadistic Cheshire.

I rise to the applause of the crowd. A nervous tic starts palpitating the left corner of my mouth, but I submit to fate and clear my throat.

"Fellow travelers," I begin, my voice cracking with a high-pitched squeak. "Fellow travelers and journeymen, the following confession will explain to you my apparent lack of fear—my mastery of serenity."

DEATH

THE ONLY ENCORE

"It was during the days preceding the Non-Ford. My first day as a leader—a wearer of the Sherpa Black Sash."

There are cries of astonishment. Then another round of cheering and applause.

"Thank you, thank you," I say in mock modesty, throwing in a few bows. "But on that first day of leadership I made a 'fatal' mistake: I misjudged the weather. Or rather, I ignored the approaching storm until it was too late.

"My companions and I were trapped on a connecting ridge three thousand feet above the nearest shelter. Open and exposed—and the lightning storm closed fast. We dropped our elevation quickly, running and stumbling down the tundra-covered slope, sending ptarmigan and marmots flapping and whistling in alarm. But the problem was that the descent route was on a collision course with the storm. The faster we descended, the sooner we were in danger.

"Lightning began flickering over neighboring ridges. Crackling thunder resounded, then rumbled off through the valley. Our only hope was to lose elevation, and lose it fast. We were fleeing for our lives, scampering down the open slope like frightened rabbits. But there was no place to hide. We were dropping all right, dropping right into the heart of the storm. Our running seemed useless as the situation grew even worse. My legs were aching, turning to rubber, cramping, stumbling and turning on rocks.

"A crackling explosion above our heads sent us sprawling flat out. The ground felt safer, but our only chance was to keep going. At least if we reached timberline we'd be relatively safe. Yet timberline was still two thousand feet below.

"We continued dropping, stumbling, fleeing for our lives, ignoring the explosions now directly above, for we knew that if we heard them then the lightning had already struck. It was when you didn't hear them, but felt

130

them, that you knew you were lost.

"Suddenly, off to the side, an alternate descent—a glacier, a snowfield, a fast glissade down to timberline. It was steep, maybe too steep. Yet the decision had been made—the problem was—not by me. The two other members were already veering off to the whiteness. And I was their leader! I would have stopped them if I was opposed, but it seemed a calculated gamble: six of one, half-a-dozen of another. The glacier was faster, but more dangerous, yet with the threat of lightning strike the open slope might be worse.

"We started our slide. The others went first. Their panic drove them careening ahead. I myself had more fear of the ice than of the storm, and so I went slower, holding back, not allowing myself to pick up much speed.

"Eventually the grade steepened. We were slipping and sliding, barely holding on. A deafening crack resounded from the ridge five hundred feet to our right. One of the members, now far below, slipped and fell. His companion stopped motionless, paralyzed, as he watched his friend sliding uncontrolled toward a rock outcrop. It meant death or certain injury, but at the last moment the imperiled member kicked off against the jagged gray boulders, glancing off as he continued his three-hundred-foot slide to the snow-chute's bottom. Within seconds it was over as quickly as it had begun. The victim slid out onto a muddy, grassy slope and stood up, waving at his companion, signaling that he was all right. And once again he sprinted off down the slope.

"We were alone. Through all the panic, the emergency, the threat of imminent disaster, I suddenly realized that we were alone. When death approaches it's each man for himself. I was the leader, and yet I was the most exposed. Neither of the two had once looked back. I could die at any moment and it would be my own fate. The shock made me slow down, made me more cautious than ever. The choice would be mine. What I did from here on out—I was solely responsible. The others had abandoned me and were themselves on their own. I would no longer try so desperately to catch up.

"Cracks of thunder exploded from the ridges on both sides, pushing me to the brink, to the limit of safety—the fine edge between my fear of falling and my fear of being struck. Involuntarily my body picked up speed, cringing and shrinking from the hovering death. My heart was pounding, adrenalin coursing, lungs laboring for air. The lightning could strike me down at any moment. The others, so far below, were now out of sight. It would be awhile before they suspected something was wrong, even longer before they subdued their panic, regained their courage and came back up.

131

And even that might be expecting too much.

"An ear-piercing crackle from above sent me sprawling and sliding out of control. I recovered by digging my heels into the snow, coming to an awkward but relieving stop. It was close—too close. I was just rising and adjusting my pack when a soft hissing filled the air. Was it the wind—the wind-blown ice crystals skimming the snow? I glanced over the glacier. The wind was blowing intermittently, but even between the gusts I could still hear a snake-like hissing from all around. And then suddenly it dawned! In horror I dropped to my knees, curling my head to the ground in a squatting fetal position. "My God!" I exclaimed. The end was near. The hissing grew louder, becoming more of a raspy rattle like a winged-insect or locust.

"The sharp, acrid smell of ozone and electricity burned the air. Was it my imagination? Was it my adrenalin? My face and hands started buzzing! My hair seemed to be bristling, standing on end! I forced myself lower into a prone position, burrowing my face into the snow. A few inches could mean the difference between life and death.

"The lightning was skittering about, taking its time, selecting its next fertile ground. An ear-shattering discharge meant the choice had been made. In a flash I was on my feet and sliding farther down the glacier. There were a few moments of safety before a new charge could be generated. I had ten or twenty clear seconds to drop as far as possible. Sliding. Slipping. Stumbling out of control. Panic drove me to my physical limit. I could be electrocuted any second. Fried to a crisp. A blind animal fear sent me careening to my doom.

"And then suddenly it dawned on me. I could die at any moment—but was this how I wanted to die—like an animal panicking and fleeing for its life—its mind filled with fear, driven in a blind frenzy. I was ashamed and embarrassed. Was this how a Warrior Sherpa would act? Is this how I wanted to pass on the legacy of my life? Is this how I wanted to be as I passed into the beyond? Had I no dignity or pride? And subtly something changed. I was still sliding down the glacier, but somehow it wasn't really me. I wasn't solely my body. Of course, I was still fleeing, but more for safety than out of fear. A drastic psychological overhaul had instantly taken place. It wasn't one individual running frantically down a mountain slope, but rather a Sherpa warrior—a wearer of the Black Sash. The feeling empowered me. I was facing death with stature. The strange thing is that objectively I was sliding just as quickly down the glacier. Perhaps even more quickly, but with more control, less desperation. And yet from the outside it probably looked the same. It was the internal that had become enlightened and transformed.

"That pretty much sums up my 'realization,' my apparent lack of fear.

For whenever I'm frenzied I calm myself by realizing that at any moment I might die. Do I want to die like a fear-crazed animal or with calmness and self-respect. I leave it to fate. If I die, I die. I take the necessary precautions, I move just as quickly, but I am more clear-headed. I am more serene."

At this the expedition has fallen into thoughtful silence, contemplating their own actions and reactions of the past.

"And what else did you find?" prompts Tensing. "How does it all end?"

"By the time I reached bottom the electric storm had already peaked. There were still rumblings through the valley, but the worst had passed. Besides, dropping below timberline made us relatively safe. The others stood awaiting me in the drizzling mist. There was embarrassment and guilt and rationalizations on all our parts. 'We thought you were right behind us!' they chimed sheepishly in excuse.

"But it didn't matter anymore. For the understanding I received transcended our transient human ordeal. I tasted what it meant to 'die like a man.' In a sense I did die, and so I have nothing more to fear. For when one faces and conquers death, nothing else can threaten or be of harm. One becomes untouchable."

"Is that all?" Tensing asks innocently. I presume he has been informed.

"Death was stalking the glacier, but luckily not for us. At the base, against an outcrop of rocks, we found the frozen body of a Sherpa. Our fears had been confirmed. They were not just the result of a frantic imagination. Death was lurking all along and we had barely escaped with our lives. What more can I say? We dragged the body into the woods and buried it. It was like burying ourselves—our fears and embarrassment, our panic and shame. In a sense it was a relief. We could now start over."

The expedition sits in silence. Each member deeply affected by my confession. Each one relating it to something in his own life. The time of intimacy is upon us. We are becoming true comrades, sharing the open wounds of life.

TREADING SOFTLY

The next day Tensing follows up my lecture on serenity with the art of serenity. He begins teaching strange, Sherpa techniques and backwoods wisdom. Supposedly this will enable us to move unobserved and undisturbed.

"You walk like elephants!" he admonishes as we tromp through some bearberry thickets. Bob is the worst. He seems to generate noise spontaneously out of nervousness. Perhaps it's his nature, perhaps he's doing his thing, but eventually he restrains himself out of consideration for us all.

Those treading the way leave no sign of their passage. No sound, no disturbance, no discernible wake. Nothing—not even the feeling that something has just passed.

DAY 74

Something has just passed. At Point Seven we all feel it simultaneously. A breeze. A shudder. And yet there is no wind. The air is still, too still, as though someone or something is watching and waiting—stalking us for some purpose we are yet to discover.

Tensing claims that the more serene one becomes, the more aware and sensitive one becomes to disruptions all around. These disturbances have always existed, but only by being quiet can they now be heard.

QUIET!

Although words can be enlivening and are sometimes essential, there are times (most times) when thoughts and words should never surface. Words break the serenity of nature. Birds and animals scurry off or stand screeching their alarm. Chances of stumbling upon or observing their natural behavior is lost.

"Quiet!" says Tensing in a hush.

"I was just thinking . . ."

"Quiet! . . . Quiet!"

For even thoughts can disrupt.

HEARING THE SILENCE

The expedition witnesses the extraordinary on Day 75. With a simple raising of his hand Tensing brings the group to a halt. We are at Glacier Lake, elevation 15,909. All motion ceases as Tensing gazes off over the black ice, anticipating something only he could feel. And then suddenly we hear it—the virtual absence of sound. In this frozen, pristine world noise does not exist. Sound and movement are smothered in a white blanket of snow. Not a bird, nor an animal, not a rustle of wind. Only the gray overcast seems to exude a dampening hiss.

That night at camp Tensing says that hearing the silence is a rare occurrence. Only at certain times of the day and year, only at certain places in the world, and only to those who are aware will total silence manifest.

STARTING OFF ON THE WRONG FOOT

The race can often be won or lost from the start. A weak or uncertain beginning casts shadows along the way. A strong or determined launch propels one through the goal.

Along the Pins and Needle traverse the expedition is exhausted on the last pitch to the summit. Step by step in spurts—half a dozen, then rest. Heart pounding. Gasping for air like a stranded fish. After a few moments I launch myself forward to the next rock, but with my back foot poised in midair, my base foot suddenly slides back along the scree. It takes all I have just to regain my balance. Adrenalin coursing, blood pounding in my brain. My entire body is jolted by the misstep.

"Go home!" Tensing chuckles off to the side.

Starting off on the right foot is a basic priority, otherwise one may as well give up.

FALSE STEPS

The "false step" is the nemesis of any serious mountaineer, for with it one loses everything that was projected as gain. Nothing is worse than stepping forward only to find one's back leg give way, or stepping forward onto a rock that topples and sends one sprawling to the ground. And even if one's balance is caught, even if one's stride is regained, too much energy and composure is lost for no purpose.

The avid climber avoids the false step at all costs, for by taking it he places his life in jeopardy. Energy required for gaining the summit needs to be conserved and fortified rather than being dissipated on an unsound base.

FALSE SUMMITS

The dreaded false summit lies in wait on the approach to the true summit. Disillusionment takes its toll both physically and mentally. One is dejected, deflated, drained of all energy. Hence, knowing the difference between true and false will eliminate deceptive hope and disappointment.

CIRCUMVENTING FALSE SUMMITS

At times it may be best to contour around a false summit, thus avoiding wasting time and energy on conquering an illusion. Sometimes, however, it may be easier to climb over and beyond the false summit, surmounting the obstacle if the effort in skirting it is too great. Experience and intuition are requisites for the successful climber.

SUPPORT

On steep inclines be careful what you grab for support. A weak limb, a loose boulder, may suddenly give way, leaving you dangling helpless in mid-air. Don't rely solely on one hand or foothold for safety. For a dead branch, a crumbling ledge, are mere flotsam on the way down.

Only life has the energy to struggle upward for growth. Death, deterioration, and debris are all too eager to descend and decay.

EASY HANDHOLDS

When ascending or descending, the perfect handhold often appears just as one is passing by. Too late! A missed opportunity. For attempting to grab the easy hold throws off timing and balance. Nevertheless, many people try for what is easy, simply because it is there. Such is human nature. The veteran climber, however, avoids at all costs the easy handhold, unless it really helps his advance.

TREASURE

Along Calico Ridge, a pegmatite dike according to Adrian, we discover an entire slope pocketed with diamonds, emeralds, and rubies. Other strange crystals and gemstones Adrian is unable to identify. They seem to be unknown rarities—a fortune in material wealth and an added scientific discovery to boot. The expedition is in a frenzy. Everything we could want all for the taking. Undreamt riches lying strewn about the ground. Frantically we hop about picking up all that we can carry, stuffing fist-sized gems into every pocket and pouch.

Tensing is amused by our antics. He stands patiently until our enthusiasm and greed subside. Guilty, embarrassed, dreading his response, the last of our pockets are finally overflowing with precious gems.

WE DISCOVER POCKETS OF CRYSTALS AND GEMS

SACRIFICE

But alas, all must be left behind. Tensing explains that at higher altitudes it will take everything we have just to carry ourselves up—not to mention the weight of our provisions and equipment. Each and every step will be a monumental struggle. Every movement a gasping effort to breathe. I consider securing only one small token specimen, but Tensing seems to have read my mind.

"Even the smallest piece can throw one off balance. At such heights timing and coordination are vital. You cannot afford the luxury of such a risk."

I therefore attempt to memorize and localize the sight. And once again Tensing seems to have read my mind.

"Our path lies forward and onward. There is no turning back. You will never pass this way again."

LOOKING BACK

An occasional glance backward along the path provides perspective. The hiker pauses in reflection over the course of his travels. However, looking backward too often can make one stumble over the present: a rock or a hole will send one sprawling to the ground. The most adept traveler thus glances back only occasionally, appreciating fully the way he has come. And yet, his presence is in the present; his vision—toward the future. In this way he is sure-footed, maintains balance, seldom falls.

Even novice mountaineers know backwards climbing is hazardous to their health.

NO RETURN

Adrian is torn by desire for the crystals. Like us, he regrets leaving them behind.

"They'd be worth a fortune back home," he remarks longingly with glazed eyes.

The expedition huddles together for warmth and confession while Tensing is out scouting the terrain. Hamel stands apart and grunts disdainfully at Adrian's comment. He is the only member unimpressed by our find. After all, what does a Barbarian need with jewels? Is it my imagination or has Hamel grown distant and moody? It seems as though he no longer belongs.

"I may be crazy," admits Bob, "but I have this funny feeling that we're never going back home."

"You too?" I query, amazed by the coincidence. "I thought it was just me—a premonition, a glimpse of the future. But somehow the past seems like a dream or another life. I can't even imagine myself back home."

Everyone shudders, for it is a confirmation of the worst. And yet we've made the choice, and this is it. We're stuck now whether we like it or not.

"Oh well," says Dave, "at least now we won't have to worry about those jewels. Where we're going they don't even matter. What does a mountain want with gems?"

DESTINATION?

"Where are we going?" asks Bob.

"No one knows," Dave replies in jest.

"Up the canyon, past the organ pipes, and then over the snow-bridge," says Adrian dryly.

"Home," grunts Hamel, gazing longingly toward the pass.

"To die," say the two kung-fu member as they practice double-kata.

"To Pochen Point!" exclaims our leader, returning unexpectedly from his survey.

THE GOAL

"Remember Pochen Point?" Tensing teases, "—that place where we're supposed to be headed. That place where you all wanted me to lead you."

"Well, where is it?" demands Adrian, still pouting about the gems. "We haven't even seen it. All I've heard is Pochen Point this, Pochen Point that. We don't even know whether or not it exists."

"We've given up everything," I lament.

"And those gems are the least of it," Adrian continues. "Why, we've given our entire lives for this fantastic goal."

"Faith," says Tensing, unruffled by our badgering. "When you commit, you must commit all the way. Don't hamper yourself with the burden of doubt. There's no place for doubt if you want to make it to the top. And besides," he adds with a knowing grin, "I've spotted Pochen Point up ahead. From now on there are no excuses. It is solely a matter of individual effort and will."

On the final approach the journey is no longer physical, but mental. And some say that on top it transforms into the spiritual.

THE NEXT BEND

Every bend in the road can lead to hope and anticipation. What vistas, what challenges, what rewards lie in wait! Are we almost there? Is it the summit? Is it camp? Is it the dreaded ford of the rushing river in the darkness of the night? Each bend in the path should fuel curiosity and wonder, energizing the traveler to explore farther along the way.

It is the weary and hopeless traveler who greets each bend with dismay. He no longer enjoys traveling. He merely stumbles along the path, verging, at any moment, on losing or abandoning the way.

A TRUE ACCOUNT

TENSING'S FIRST ORDEAL OF SHERPAHOOD

Realizing that the expedition has lost its vision, Tensing relates an episode that will shock us back to our senses. He also believes that we've become grounded. "You're leadfooted," he rebukes us. "You need a dose of the ethereal." He then proceeds to impart a sense of Sherpa nobility.

"My first test of Sherpahood was to lead members of your world to the summit of what they considered the highest mountain. I told their leader that this was not necessarily the highest mountain, but when he asked me what was, I told him Pochen Point. The fellow just laughed it off as a joke. Oh well, the climb made history in your world, whereas in ours it was scarcely a passing joke. What's funny is that no one seems to know who reached the summit first. So now, I'll reveal what really happened on top."

Though both of us were exhausted and could barely move our feet, the moment we sighted the summit we became revitalized and inspired. Both of us were eager to burst forth to the top, but just as suddenly we both became restrained and subdued.

"You first," said your leader.

"No, no—after you. You are the leader. It is only right that you should be first."

"But you were our guide," he insisted. "Without your knowledge and Sherpa wisdom we wouldn't even be here. And besides, you're native to this country, and a native, not a foreigner, should be the first on top."

"But you organized the expedition," I countered. "Without your initiative there would be no climb."

"Well," he said with resolve. "It seems obvious what we should do."

He knelt down and was busy doing something by his side. Suddenly, a snowball came flying into my face. It stung like hell.

"Why did you do that, crazy westerner!"

I made a snowball in self-defense and flung it back. We flung and slung icy snowballs back and forth until our energy was drained and we stood exhausted, ready to collapse.

"Shall we?" he asked innocently, extending his hand. Arm-in-arm, hand-in-hand, we climbed atop the highest crest.

THE MOUNTAIN OF LIFE

Tensing explains that the mountain has always been a spiritual symbol. Every culture has held it in awe and reverence. And every society has considered mountain-climbers with respect. For the mountain is an archetype within man's collective psyche.

"Look at it in this way," says Tensing. "Climbing a mountain is a task that challenges the body, mind, and spirit, bringing them together at a single place in space and time. On the summit, mind, body, and spirit are unified the moment one touches the highest point."

"Looked at geometrically, the mountain can be viewed as a cone. It then becomes obvious that, regardless of the approach taken (as long as one keeps climbing), one will eventually reach the same point at the top. For this reason each person's way is as valid as any other. It is merely a matter of preference, a personal choice of paths. Some may be easier or more difficult, some longer and some shorter. But the end point for everyone is always the same. The summit is what brings all and everything together."

ALL PATHS ARE ONE PATH

On approaching the summit the way becomes clear. The closer to the top, the less obscure the path. One emerges from the tangled undergrowth out of the darkness of the forest.

The higher one travels, the less alternatives, the less confusion. For near the top all paths merge and coalesce until finally, at the summit, they all become one.

FOLLOW THE LEADER

On the Organ Pipes Adrian nearly leads us to our doom. At his insistence, despite the objections of others, we ascend a narrow chimney onto a wind-swept, knife-edge ridge. Bit by bit we pick our way over the serrated pinnacles, clinging spread-eagle to vertical faces, scampering over rotten ledges as they crumble and break away. Eventually, after two nightmarish hours, the sky darkens as we come to a sheer thousand foot drop. We could go no farther. We would have to turn back. But a sudden hailstorm sends lightning flickering about the ridge. The rocks become coated with a hazardous film of ice. No one dares move. The expedition is immobilized. We are stranded at 19,000 feet.

Luckily the storm breaks as quickly as it began. The sun shines through, melting the ice and allowing us to traverse and backtrack down the chimney. No casualties are suffered, but we had risked our lives to no avail. The toll is upon the energy and morale of the expedition.

"I told you so," rings through everyone's mind.

Bob laughs maniacally while Dave just shakes his head and grins. Everyone else mulls about in exasperation.

"Gentlemen," admonishes Tensing, "following a leader is a matter of choice. Don't blame the leader if he leads you astray, for his choice is in fact the choice of all. Taking comfort in 'I told you so,' does no good if you're dead. At the turning point, you hold your life in your own hands. Scrambling over a knife-edge when you're suffering fatigue, glissading down an ice field that's a little too steep. To be able to say 'he made me' makes little difference when you fall."

On the top one must indeed follow oneself. For ultimately there is no one to fall back on or to blame.

THE METAPHYSICAL MOUNTAIN

No one blames Adrian outright and so Adrian must blame himself.

"I could have sworn it was the way I went up before." Adrian scratches his head in consternation, searching for an answer. "Continental drift?" he asks Tensing hopefully.

Tensing just grins.

"More like high-altitude senility," I chide, "lack of oxygen to the brain. It's why climbers are often at a loss for words. The exhilaration is breathtaking—literally."

The expedition is amused and tongue-tied. No one says a word. Finally Tensing breaks the tension.

"It is the same mountain," he acknowledges. "Your memory is correct."

"Then where did I go wrong? Did the mountains change overnight?"

Tensing smiles and shakes his head. "For what you have achieved there are no words." Everyone becomes silent and respectful. The expedition borders on reverence. "All right, all right," concedes Tensing, "there are words."

"What you have done is tampered with the metaphysical. You have climbed so many mountains that they gradually seemed the same. All your memories fused into the memory of one single mountain—an archetypal mountain. This mountain, composed of every mountain, was the only mountain you had ever climbed—the only mountain you will ever climb. That's why your memory became confused. You touched base, for a moment, with the eternal. And in that moment every approach was seemingly the way. You could have even imagined a route and it would have miraculously appeared—because every mountain is simply a variant of the One."

"Then why didn't the route go? Why were we left hanging?"

"Because the other members of the expedition simply no longer believed. And, sensing their dismay, you yourself no longer believed. When the last glimmer of hope was extinguished, the abyss suddenly appeared. The expedition found itself metaphysically cliffed-out."

LEADING YOURSELF

A point is reached in a follower's life when it is time for him to lead. The student has progressed to the level of teacher. To remain a student leads only to immaturity and regression. To become a teacher leads to further growth and refinement. To lead is to see clearly for the first time, unbeclouded by the dust of those ahead.

"Upon the heights one must learn the Sherpa art of leadership—even if it be only the leading of oneself."

UPON THE HEELS

Tensing admonishes us to be weaned and acquire independence, but the path becomes narrower, steeper, and more hazardous. The situation comes to a head on Left-Hand Pass—so-called for its uncanny reversals of approach. Because of its trickiness the expedition follows close at heels—each person frantically keeping pace with the one in front. Eyes forward, glued upon the rocky terrain. A false handhold, a misstep could send one plummeting into the abyss, and so each member follows closely behind. Too closely, for on a narrow reversed precipice Tensing stops suddenly, and those behind jam together nearly sending him off the edge.

"All right! That's it!" he stomps his foot upon the crumbling ledge. "From now on, you're on your own. You know the way—you always have. I'll follow behind just to make sure no one gives up."

DAY 91

On Agorn Pass we scale the loftiest peak thus far—all without knowing the supposed difficulty involved. Afterwards, on the crossover, we take readings and check references.

"That was S-2!" exclaims Adrian.

"No way!" I say.

"It can't be," argues Bruce.

Then we all fall silent as Dave calculates the coordinates and agrees. To our amazement we have completed the final stretch of our journey, surmounting with comparable ease the most challenging test. With a twinkle in his eye, Tensing confirms our unwitting victory—a case in point that, with committed effort, most obstacles are not as arduous as they seem.

MIND SETS

OR

"Sermon On How To Mount"

"It's all a matter of altitude," explains Adrian to the dumbfounded expedition. We nod dumbly as he corrects himself. "I mean 'aptitude'!" he falters. "I mean 'attitude'!" he slurs with hypoxia.

Tensing takes over the sermonizing while Adrian unclogs his garbled mouth with a refreshing swig of sour, yak milk.

"Your mental framework comprises ninety percent of the climb. Gear up, anticipate a challenge, and the most rugged mountain is scaled with ease. But lie back, take things for granted, and the simplest ascent becomes a monumental struggle. The old adage 'prepare for the worst' originated from the climb and, applied mercilessly, will render any object surmountable."

THE INITIATION

Tensing Explains Further

At high-altitude camp a yak-dung fire is built and Tensing resumes his life's saga. The expedition huddles in joyful anticipation.

"As a novice Sherpa I dreaded the eventual period of initiation—the study and preparation, the rituals and grueling testing. I envisioned a nightmarish three-day marathon examination. I listened with morbid curiosity to stories of past initiations—students passing out, vomiting, and giving up. Rumors of sickness, madness and death.

"And then suddenly, without warning, one day at practice I was called before the assembly. The Head Sherpa was holding the distinguished black sash draped formally across his outstretched arms. The Abbot entered the hall and the assembly bowed prostrate as he seated himself upon the low platform.

" 'Tensing Sherpa,' he barked out with military gruffness. I stepped forward at once, rising nervously before the assembly. 'Through diligence, knowledge, and years of discipline.' He signaled to the Head Sherpa who placed the black sash over the Abbot's arms. 'The Tao-Tsing Monastery offers you the Sherpa sash of honor.'

"I was stunned, shocked in disbelief. Where was the testing—the dread and anxiety? The Abbot then draped the sash ceremoniously over my shoulder. The Head Sherpa called attention as the teachers and I exchanged bows. I turned to the assembly. Attention was called and for the first time my former fellow-initiates and I exchanged bows."

"And thus it was," says Tensing as we sit huddled around the fire "that my life's hardest challenge was met and overcome on its own."

Each Day is the Test

If embraced fully then every day one will do one's best. Seemingly insurmountable obstacles will be overcome with ease.

IN THE DARK

"But I thought you said we would be climbing S-2 in the dark," Bob asks dumbfounded.

Everyone looks at Bob as though he's an idiot.

"We did climb it in the dark," scolds Adrian.

"But I like night-climbing. I thought it would be fun."

"Well, I'll tell you what," Adrian replies in exasperation. "Tonight, when we're all asleep, why don't you sneak back and re-climb it by yourself?"

"All right!" cheers Bob, totally delighted.

AN EXTRACT FROM BOB'S JOURNAL

(Found upon the summit marker of S-2)

Recorded by moonlight on Agorn Pass as I attempt to scale S-2 in the dark.

They will say I am crazy, but only history can judge. Be it through intuition or dream, but I am certain that S-2 is in reality Pochen Point. Or rather, that what is taken as S-2 is actually higher than its famous neighbor Pochen Point. It is common knowledge that without extensive surveys slight elevation differences are impossible to judge. It is also known that atmospheric illusions caused by light-scattering often make a lower point seem high and a higher farther point seem low. I have therefore taken it upon myself to scale S-2 by night and survey by moonlight when such disturbances are minimal. Besides, Pochen Point, if it does in fact exist, was hidden in cloud cover while we were previously upon S-2. Such cloud cover dissipates at night so that a clear sighting should be possible. If S-2 is really Pochen Point then a revaluation is necessary. The expedition would in fact already be over.

BOB'S NIGHT OUT

Neither Dave nor I knew what was in store for us on S-2. Neither of us anticipated the magnitude or the consequences. To us it was just another typical climb—perhaps a little harder or more complicated, but nothing too far from the ordinary.

We started the way we always started our little adventures. Packed the previous day. Ready to leave after work. Driving through the night to the trailhead where we would make camp and begin climbing first thing in the morning. We had five days off—just enough to escape the routine and frantic pace of civilization. We would be isolated on back roads thirty miles from the nearest highway. The farthest and most isolated we had ever been.

I didn't realize anything was wrong until it was far too late. The understanding came slowly, gradually building to a crescendo that would culminate in outright panic. The first inkling came when Dave told me we needed gas.

"How come you didn't fill up the day before like you always do?" I asked, thumping my feet on the floor and flailing my arms in agitation.

"Thought it would be better to fill up on the way. That way we'll have a fuller tank in the back country."

Sounded logical to me so I got down from the headrest. Dave always was one for logic and doing things right. Think ahead: that was his motto. I was the one people thought of as flippant and crazy. But who was careless this time? From the start I had the feeling something was wrong, and my left foot knew it. It kept thumping up and down with a life of its own.

The wrongness grew worse. Although the map showed several towns along the route, we were traveling late at night and on a secondary highway. In each town we passed through the gas stations were closed. The fuel gauge was dropping. And our last hope for salvation went by like the rest. It wasn't even a town, but merely a junction with "no services."

I was driving by then, for we had switched to relieve monotony, though monotony was the furthest thing from my mind. Anxiety was a far more apt description. Dave and I were craning our necks at the fuel gauge, estimating and calculating whether there was enough for the backwoods. Entering was no problem. It was getting back out that was tricky. I didn't dare stop to discuss the situation, for stopping meant wasting gas idling on the side of the road, or turning off the engine and wasting even more on the start-up.

I slowed and coasted without stepping on the brakes. We were, after all, on an isolated highway—no one behind or ahead of us in sight.

"So what do you think?" we both chimed nearly simultaneously.

"I don't know. What do you think?"

"I asked you first."

"I asked you second."

"Don't play games," Dave said in exasperation. "I'm serious. This could mean trouble." Dave had a knack for understatement.

Being one for cheerfulness and levity I played the part. "I'll bet we can make it. Besides, the worst that could happen is that we'll become stranded and die."

But Dave, the straight man, had to calculate to the meticulous. "Let's see, the turnoff is ten miles farther, then it's thirty miles in. That's forty miles both ways. The needle is at one-quarter: that means two and a half gallons. At thirty-five miles to the gallon we should have plenty, especially since the reserve holds at least one or two gallons more. That's just about right to get us to the next town on the way out."

"If we come out during the day," I needled his memory.

"Okay, okay. No need to rub it in. So we're agreed. We keep going."

We kept going. And right away I knew something was wrong.

"Dave," I chirped timidly. "Is it my imagination or does the needle seem to be dropping faster than normal?" Dave leaned over the steering column.

"By golly!" he exclaimed. "It must be both our imaginations. It can't be real. It's our psychological perspective."

My feet began thumping. I suddenly felt the urge to urinate. And my arms started flailing wildly about.

"Do you mind?" said Dave calmly.

"But Dave, I swear, the needle was exactly at one-quarter. Now look how far it's dropped. Maybe we're leaking gas."

"Do you want to stop and check?" Dave challenged.

The car kept going. My foot kept thumping. And both of us were eyeing the gauge twenty times a minute.

"Drive slower," said Dave urgently.

"What for?" I nearly screamed.

"If you drive slower we won't use as much gas."

"But you just said we had plenty."

"If you didn't drive so fast we would. Just slow down so we don't take any chances."

We were now taking chances. I slowed, but that was the worst thing to do. Driving was now agony. Time was drawn out and every moment was a painstaking crawl down the road. The longer the engine ran, wouldn't it be using more gas? Wouldn't it be better to drive full speed to our destination and then turn it off? But logic won out and so we strained and struggled, pushing the car along by sheer mental exertion and will.

Driving slower at least provided an opportunity to view the scenery. At least the little that was illuminated by the bright lights of the car. There was nothing else to do to pass the time. Normally we zipped by so fast that everything was a blur. Now the landscape stood out in relief—three-dimensional and real with detail and contrast, not a two-dimensional streaming, formless cloud.

"You know," I said to voice what we both were thinking, "it sure looks weird out there."

"I know," agreed Dave, "I was just thinking the same thing. I've been down nearly every highway around. This is probably the only one I've missed. My God, it looks like another world."

"Look at the size of those cacti."

"And those giant sage brush."

"And those things we don't even know the name of!"

"What's happening!"

"It's like the twilight zone."

"It's like we're in a dream."

I wanted to screech on the brakes. But the car kept moving, inevitably, inexorably with a will of its own.

We turned off the main highway onto the isolated gravel road. We were entering the back country. There was no turning back now.

"Slow down," Dave said in panic, craning his neck at the gas gauge. "Maybe we should turn back now."

"What for?" I laughed maniacally. "We have enough to make it."

"Stop the car!" Dave demanded, flipping on the overhead dome-light. He scanned the maps and reconsidered. "We might just have enough. It's borderline. What the heck, live dangerously," he relented, flipping off the light and collapsing into his seat.

"Oh God," Dave moaned, shaking his head in hopelessness. We were entering another world, isolating ourselves from civilization. No help or assistance would come our way. We were on our own. If we broke down, if we ran out of gas, it might be days before anyone passed our way.

The road degenerated. From gravel it turned to dirt, then mudholes and boulders. We forded streams that rose to the bottom of the door.

"All right!" we cheered as we made it to the other side, but really it was the strained laughter of anxiety. We didn't know what we were doing or what we were getting into, but it was too late now. Things could only grow worse.

"God!" Where's the other road? We've missed the turnoff."

"But there wasn't one," I objected.

"There has to be. The map shows it. We must be on the wrong road. We're going the wrong way. Stop the car!" Dave yelled as I slammed on the brakes.

"But there's no other road," I argued. "It has to be right. When there's only one choice it must be correct."

Dave remained unconvinced, flipping on the dome-light, shuffling through books and maps, banging his head, cursing, and then finally giving in. We could only go forth. There was no other way.

"It's all wrong," Dave mumbled. "We're lost. We're going to die."

"What's that?" Dave screamed. Up ahead fantastic creatures flared in the headlights.

"Ghostly white cows as big as our car. Makes sense," Dave shuddered.

Other figures loomed up, but vanished into the darkness. They were large and hairy, loping upright with big feet. A giant bird like a pterodactyl swooped down and over the cliff. We were winding our way up into the heart of the Magic Mountains, hoping to God that we were on the right path. At mile thirty we stopped, not because we wanted to, but because we had to.

"We can't go any farther," Dave said, checking the odometer. "We'll never make it out unless we stop right here."

"But this isn't the place," I objected. "Everything's wrong. Come on, Dave, just a little farther. Just around the next bend in the road."

But the next bend was even worse. We weren't even facing the right direction. Where S-2 should have been was only a pasture and rolling hills. The high points and escarpments were totally reversed. Either the maps were in error or we were nowhere near the trailhead.

"Let's just stop," Dave insisted. "In the morning we'll be able to figure out where we are. We're just getting lost and using up gas."

I slowed and backed the car onto a narrow pullout. The cliff ledge was barely two feet away. I cut the engine and lights and a host of shadows loomed out of nowhere. The darkness flared up silhouetting the night. We were engulfed by a sudden silence and stillness. It reverberated through the car, pressuring and hissing in our ears. With the heater off, the coldness quickly seeped inward. Either the night was invading, or we were merging into the wilderness.

"God, I'm freezing. And it's supposed to be summer. I didn't bring any heavy clothes, did you?"

"I didn't even bring my sleeping bag," I shuddered. "I was counting on just sleeping out under the stars."

"We won't even be able to sleep inside at this rate."

"Maybe we can turn on the heat," I joked. For the more the car ran, the less gas we'd have to get back. And so Dave and I just settled into our seats for the night. Surprisingly, after a few hours of shivering and cursing, we grew numb and relaxed enough to let go of our misery and fall asleep.

It was near dawn when I first heard the music—a tinkling and clinking of silvery bells or wind chimes. Dave was sound asleep, and so I opened the door quietly and tiptoed outside. That's when I saw the lights up ahead. The parking lot and what looked to be a restaurant or gift shop. We were almost there! I would surprise Dave by climbing to the summit while he slept. Besides, there might be hot coffee and donuts to bring back. Dave would like that, I know he would. And maybe they would even have some gas.

I took a shortcut up an immaculate private drive cobbled with beautiful, multicolored stones. Tiny mushroom lamps and richly ornate figurines decorated the path.

"Wait up!" cried a voice from beyond. It was Tensing—my old dance instructor from Fairview High. "Are you sure this is what you want?" he asked while limping up to greet me.

"Of course, who wouldn't? Fresh donuts, hot coffee, a summit seat to witness the rising sun."

"Then, by all means, let's go, count me in!" he cheered as we hurried up the path to that pie-in-the-sky donut shop at the top of the world . . .

BREAKDOWN

"Bob's gone!" Dave hollers with the dawning of first light.

The camp stirs to life from the sluggishness of bizarre dreams. It is the beginning of the end. We are panicking, jumping about as if someone has called "fire!"

"Hamel's gone!" yells Adrian.

"And Tensing, too," I add as serenely as possible.

"What the hell's happening?" Dave asks while pulling on his boots.

The kung-fu members start punching and kicking each other.

"Maybe it's a test," suggests Adrian. "Maybe Tensing wants to see what we're really made of."

"Or maybe it's real," Dave counters. "Maybe they're really in trouble!"

"What should we do?" they ask in unison, turning to me.

"Me!" I scream, totally distraught. With Tensing gone why should I be in charge?

The drawback of relying too fully upon a leader: when the leader weakens so does everyone else. When he is missing all progress comes to a halt.

LOYALTY

Dave realizes what has happened, what he must now do.

"Bob accepted Adrian's challenge. He tried climbing S-2 in the dark. I've got to go back. I've got to find him before it's too late."

No room exists for reconsideration or debate. Dave's mind is made up and he will not relent.

"You may be forgoing Pochen Point," Adrian reminds. "The climbing season is coming to a close. Favorable weather is almost over."

"Can't be helped," says Dave. "I'll find him or his body if it's the last thing I ever do." Dave has packed and is ready to leave.

"Pochen Pass—the Bears' Playground," I inform him just in case. "Rendezvous day after tomorrow at dusk and we'll set up base camp."

But as Dave departs we feel he will never again be seen.

Loyalty, heroism, self-sacrifice.

On the downslope of K-7 (the sight of my near-death with lightning) I remember stumbling upon a mother ptarmigan and her brood. She squawked and fluttered about feigning injury or a broken wing. All the while leading us farther away from her nest, tempting us, luring us, just beyond reach, endangering her life, ready to sacrifice herself for the safety of her offspring.

As we watch Dave vanish into the tundra-covered slopes of S-2 we witness a true embodiment of Sherpa nobility.

COMMANDEERING

"Tracks!" yells Adrian from across the camp. "Yeti footprints!" The kung-fu members stop their fighting. We all run and gather around Hamel's bedroll. Sure enough, enormous hairy footprints cover the moist earth. They lead off up a ridge to the plateau on the right.

"Yeti!" we all shudder in alarm.

"I never thought they were real," Adrian shakes his head in disbelief.

But there it is before us. Hamel has been captured by a myth and it is up to us to find him. We break camp and follow the orderly progression of tracks. Around the next hillock we catch sight of our objective: a group of dark, massive figures silhouetted by the first light. They are a formation, a flight pattern across the alpine terrain. And they move like lightning, loping up the slope like mountain lions or snow leopards. But where is Hamel? At this distance his form is indistinguishable from the rest. We take it for granted, a matter of faith, that he is there.

CHALLENGE

Two hours have passed and we are no closer to catching up. It takes all we have just to keep pace. And the Yeti are unconcerned that they are being followed. If they cared, we would certainly be left in the dust.

They are formidable. Truly worthy opponents—driven by a force, a vision we cannot comprehend. The expedition may well be outmatched. Watching their graceful, naturally undulating strides and comparing them to our own stilted, jerky steps, I know in my heart that they will never be caught. At the moment we must be satisfied just keeping them in sight. For only with luck or by fate can they possibly be overcome.

OVERCOMING ONESELF

Who are we trying to overcome? Is it the Yeti? Or are the Yeti merely a figment of our mind? Are they a reflection of what needs to be overcome within ourselves?

We follow all day, barely keeping them in sight. In fact, although we are giving it our best, the Yeti are gradually outdistancing us over time. In the late afternoon sun, the formation of dark figures slips uniformly over the ridge onto the plateau. They are out of sight and we are lagging far behind. In my heart I know that the Yeti have won, Hamel will never again be seen. It is mere formality and pride that keep us tracking up the slope.

Near dusk the expedition slips over the ridge onto the plateau. To our surprise we are confronted by a vast intermountain lake—a lake so large and undulating that it is almost a sea. Large, murky waves roll and break against the shore. In the dusk the darkening water becomes ominous. It is as though the expedition has been transported through time—gazing out over a primordial ocean. We are awestruck, standing in silence, witnessing the mesmerizing roll and breaking of each wave along the sandy beach. In the gloomy depths I catch glimpses of unnamed prehistoric shapes—animals, fish and reptiles that even the imagination cannot recognize.

TRANSCENDENCE AT PYRAMID LAKE

The Yeti have vanished. But it no longer matters. Even Adrian seems to have forgotten Hamel and become serene.

"Maybe they led us here on purpose," he says with tears in his eyes.

The brisk breeze, the smell of brine, the roar and clash of the waves. It is becoming chilly with the oncoming darkness of the setting sun. But we are transfixed by the moment, the power of the spectacle, the image that holds us motionless in awe. There is nothing else that we can do, nothing else we want to do.

Above the dark, restless sea the purple sky is tinged with splashes of orange and red clouds. The sun is offering its last fiery display of light. Out of its ochre furnace dark specks gradually emerge—a formation of large birds gliding smoothly above the sea. We are unnerved as they grow in size and sail overhead. Slowly they turn and circle back in search of prey. With long legs draped back and wide, angular wings that flap and glide, their silhouettes are uncannily those of prehistoric pterodactyls. The expedition is enraptured as the flying animals break formation, dipping and soaring among the primordial waves.

In our hearts we will never leave this mystic sea.

VERBAL DOUBLE-KATA

The Kung-fu Members Explain Their Movements

"Conquering the enemy is easy.
Conquering oneself is hard."

The expedition recovers its senses, passes back through time, climbs to the level of the Neenan Traverse to make camp. Bruce and Lee sidle off to do kata when Adrian finally throws down his gauntlet.

We have heard fragments of Tensing's life, dreamt of Bob's night out, embraced my near-death with lightning, glimpsed Hamel's Yeti mysticism at Pyramid Lake. But what of the kung-fu artists? They keep to themselves, practicing every chance they get. Mysterious and inscrutable. Dedicated, resilient, they train incessantly day and night perfecting their art. But what is it all for? What does it all mean? At Neenan Crossing Encampment Adrian challenges them for an accounting. Their answer is itself a verbal demonstration, an interaction, a melding of two forces into a whole. One verbalizes while the other dramatizes. As one philosophizes the other harmonizes life.

LIFE — KATA ULTIMA

In the oriental tradition of martial arts a "kata" is a form of prearranged fighting movements. The pattern is ancient, describing an imaginary battle with various opponents. The pseudo-fights often depict a master's actual encounter hundreds of years past in some distant land. Other times it is simply a series of fighting techniques designed by the master in the most suitable form.

The purpose of the kata is to facilitate a student's learning. By practicing each movement as though in actual combat, the student learns the practical application of each technique. It is not an imaginary series of isolated techniques, but rather a logical progression of defensive-offensive movements in real life. The movements make sense. The student can see them applied.

Katas vary in both length and style. A kung-fu kata may last ten seconds. A tai-chi kata may last an hour. Katas can thus be found within totally different martial arts—karate, kung-fu, ju-jitsu, aikido. And varying systems of katas can be found within each art. In kung-fu one can specialize in any number of different styles. One can study the white crane, the dragon, the praying mantis, or the phoenix. Bizarre and esoteric systems such as stone-hand, iron-hand, and poison-hand exist.

Each kata must be practiced diligently until it becomes perfect. One must perform a kata at least a thousand times before one can even begin to know it. A thousand times: once a day for the next three years. And even then the kata is not yet perfect, the form not even close to being mastered.

"I remember a time in my life of hard, manual labor. Day after day digging ditches in the sun, shoveling gravel, chopping weeds, and laying sod. Ten hours a day. Six days a week. Over and over without any rest. Monotonous and trivial. Repetition without end. An eternal cycle of meaningless fatigue."

Repetition is necessary. Each movement must be practiced again and again—each time more accurate, closer to perfection. And each repetition must be practiced as though it were the first. No matter how boring, each repetition must be new, with the clarity and anticipation of a first attempt. Only then will the kata come to life. Only then will the student attain perfection.

> "I remember wondering to myself what it was all for. Where did it all lead? Eating. Sleeping. Working. Eating. Sleeping. Working. Day in and day out. Time after time. It all seemed so futile. Every action so mundane."

The student must be conscious of every movement—continuously aware of the present moment. Focus, speed, power, and timing all blend into one effective move. But eventually, with repetition, performance and performer merge. Each movement becomes interrelated with the next, making a whole of the kata rather than just isolated parts. The student is no longer consciously aware of his actions. The kata has been assimilated. Kata and student are one.

> "I remember the dream—working and sweating in the hot sun. And yet each movement was perfect. Each action intentionally designed. There was no wasted effort. No loss of momentum. Each task flowed with total ease. There was a joy in the release of energy. A carefree indulgence in the physical moment. The movement of a shovel. The crusty penetration of the earth. A light scratching of a rake dusting the topsoil for stones. The smell of fresh sod newly unrolled. The simplest act meaningfully inscribed upon the world. And yet it was accomplished so quickly, so efficiently— without complaint."

The Tao has no complaint, neither should a man. Every action, every repetition should be done with innocence. A spontaneous affirmation from

180

moment to moment. Each moment being real—never a reflection of the past. To begin a kata is to begin a new life. Each kata is itself the creation of the world.

"And I began to see each and every movement as real. Every action and inaction was imbued with meaning. Every word spoken and withheld had had its effect. It was like a game. An infinite game. A world championship of the moment. Existence itself was its own challenge.

"I remember the series of occurrences that had brought me here—the movement through the streets, the choice of paths, each moment infinitely broken down to an alternative. The stranger who had smiled. The dog that had barked. The squirrel that had scampered before me in fright. It was all significant. Each decision branched into myriad choices. Each moment was another universe—burdening or enlightening to each one's taste. And then oneself. One's responses! That smile of my own. That girl in the café. And the dreams. And the fantasies. Progressing forever. Interacting. Disintegrating. Assimilating. Correlating. An infinite series of lines and forces intersecting at one point and then diverging—emerging and blossoming into life. I was walking, flowing within this river of chance, gracefully attuned to the undulations. Swirling about the eddies and flung off into the mainstream, gliding and churning over rapids and boulders. It was a movement to rejoice, a sacred dance of life."

Each kata is alive. Each form has its own rhythm. With repetition the kata gradually comes to life. The original pulse of the ancestors is re-awakened. One is moving in tune with ancient battles, practicing alongside ancestral ghosts, flowing with the ever-flowing Tao.

The energy can be sensed. It is the "ki" or "chi" that vitalizes life. It is the "ether" through which the universe flows. The kata is merely a vehicle for tapping this source. It is a mechanism through which to engage the divine.

"I was passing day by day. A simple walk to work. Feet forward. Alternate. Light hop onto curb. Sparrows chirping, pecking, heads bobbing. Wind blowing. Trees swaying. Scattered leaves. Legs moving. Arms swinging. Blue skies. Sunny day. People talking. Music playing. Lights changing, traffic merging, flowing in a mechanical river of life. Nodding heads. Smiles. Eyes turned—engaged. Laughter. Again. And walking. Rhythmic swinging. Spiral staircase, and sidestepping, averting. Smiling. Semi-circle and wave. Feet forward. And greetings. And turning. And chatting. And the clock ticking away. And life passing by. And the work. And the sun. And the earth. And the stars . . ." *

----

*In oriental folklore and mysticism the movements of a man from birth to death trace out an intricate pattern unique to each soul. Whether clumsy or graceful, natural or contrived, each movement is etched onto the eternal canvas. This is the reason for the oriental deliberateness of character. Each action is seen as unique and irrevocable. Once done the pattern is set. Once moved the movement is complete. The sum tracings of a man from birth to death mark out a figure so complex that only the Tao can conceive it. Such a divine figure is said to be that of one's Self. Such a series of intricate movements—Kata Ultima—the sacred, ever-flowing kata of life.

LIFE DANCE

"Tensing."

"Tensing who?"

"Tensing Sherpa."

"Yes, Master. I'm here, Master."

"Tensing Sherpa—wake up!"

"I am awake, Master."

"Tensing Sherpa—bearer of the White Sash, Leader of the Borgonian Expedition to Pochen Point. You may now perform your dance."

"But how can I dance with a broken leg?"

TENSING WHO

No one knows anything of Tensing. Where did he come from? Who engaged him? Where is he now? Indeed, we can scarcely recall his features. His presence, his memory fade dimly into the past. Did he ever really exist? Was he a necessary projection, an hallucination, a focal point to guide us through each day?

"I remember something of Tensing," says Adrian, racking his memory. "Wasn't he the weird guy who kept promising to tell his story and to perform a dance? Didn't he tell parts of his story each day?"

"His story was each day," I suddenly realize. It dawns on me that Tensing's life was the story. "And his dance—that strange dance with all its peculiar gyrations and graceful flow—that dance was actually the dance of life."

Tensing's movements are complete. Gracefully he bows out and we are now on our own.

"Remember what they say," Adrian cautions, "you should never travel alone."

"At the top, one must always travel alone, even if someone happens to be along."

THE TRAVELER

Village after village. One person after another. Traveling through the endless cycles of life. I am a drifter shifting from one scene to another, realizing only now that all that I have is my goal.

DAY 106

And yet, Pochen Point no longer matters. I am no longer in a rush. The daily routines are taken one at a time. Day by day.

"If one looks at life as a journey from birth to death then the way one travels is all that matters."

DAY 107

The following morning we break camp and attempt the Neenan Crossing Traverse. But the expedition is in a quandary. The snow bridge is nearly collapsing. The ice face we must climb over is beginning to melt. A dangerous crossing under normal conditions is now almost suicidal. Yet there is no other way. To climb Pochen Point we must traverse.

"Is it worth it?" asks Lee, expressing everyone's doubts.

The climbing season was technically over. By all rights we should return. Sanity demanded that we return. But Pochen Point compelled insanity, for the legendary mountain could be scaled only once every twenty years. Only one season in twenty allowed a favorable approach.

"If we don't do it now, when will we ever do it?" asks Adrian.

"We can't possibly turn back after all we've given up," I maintain.

"It may not even be possible to turn back," says Bruce, "much less have the energy or desire to return for another attempt."

"Then it's decided," I conclude. "We cross over. Who goes first?"

Each member of the expedition stands looking at me.

LEADERSHIP

"But why me?" I say to myself. Luckily I say nothing to the others. Instead I begin scoping out the best route to traverse.

It was the problem of leadership and the group had chosen me. The leader had to be dauntless, show courage and fortitude. He was an example for each member to emulate. Once he surmounted an obstacle all others would be inspired and follow suit. It would be easy if shown easy, hard if shown hard. I had to succeed, for the fate of the expedition now rested upon my shoulders. The fulfillment of our collective dream was now up to me.

CROSSOVER

"The Neenan Crossing Traverse"—the words echo through my mind, reverberate through my being. The very mention of it sends chills through even veteran climbers. Even the most experienced hold Neenan Crossing in awe. I can now see why. The hair-raising stories told around campfires fail to do justice to the traverse. It is the most horrifying prospect I have ever encountered. A sheer vertical wall of rock and ice forty feet long. Forty feet of inch-by-inch, spread-eagled clinging to frozen granite. One misstep spells disaster. One false grip means the end.

I begin shaking involuntarily. Heart pounding. Heavy breathing. A cold sweat beads my forehead as I gaze down to where I will fall. An animal fear paralyzes my body. Blind panic grips my soul. My life, my death, the choice lay before me. By chance or by fate one or the other would be mine.

A BRIEF RESPITE

"But wait a second," says Adrian. I am ready to collapse with relief. "Don't I get a chance to tell my story?" The expedition eagerly gathers around, secretly embracing this temporary escape.

"I'm sure you've all wondered about my life," he says smugly, "what makes me what I am, why I am different from the others."

The members of the expedition look at each other and shake their heads. We shrug our shoulders with indifference. Why should we be curious about Adrian?

Adrian is taken aback.

"Well I'll tell you anyway, seeing as how we're all going to die."

At 26,700 feet the expedition settles down for the final installment.

ADRIAN'S OBSESSION

In Quest of the Absolute

"Over here!" she called out from the top of the craggy sub-peak. "It's this way!" Her voice chimed in the brisk air, her brown hair fluttering with each gust and breeze.

It was a bright, clear day perfect for mountaineering. Low cloud banks were forming off the horizon, but they were too far distant to be of much concern. We had the entire afternoon to loiter about. And yet a chilling wind was buffeting the exposed summit, urging us to keep moving just to stay warm. It was no place to linger. And besides, it was better to get going, for we were attempting the dreaded knife-edge to Desolation Peak—a crossing that had claimed dozens of lives in the past. The last thing needed was pressure from either time or an incoming storm. What was needed was calmness and composure in order to deal with the unexpected.

For us this was the culmination of our mountaineering. We had never climbed anything nearly as difficult and dangerous, nor were we likely to do so in the future. The Desolation Traverse was the furthest we were willing to go. In all practicality it was the last obstacle in our lives.

WARNING!

Climbing in the Borgonian Mountains should be attempted only by experienced, well-equipped parties. The nature of the steep rugged terrain, sudden lightning storms, and falling rocks have caused the deaths of even the most experienced climbers. In one summer alone five people died on Desolation Peak in separate, unrelated accidents. Never climb alone. Tell someone where you are going. And be aware of the warning symptoms of hypothermia, altitude sickness, and Borgonian mountain madness.

"Are you sure you want to do this?" I asked, giving her an option to back out.

"Sure I'm sure. Don't you?"

"It looks pretty steep. We can always go back the way we came, skip the traverse, and climb Desolation from the easier red couloir another day."

"But it doesn't look that bad," she insisted. "We can at least try and if it's too hard we can always turn back. The weather is perfect. Besides, the guidebook says only the first three hundred feet are difficult, from then on it's smooth sailing."

Of all Borgonian passages the Desolation Peak Traverse must rank as the worst. When campfires are dying, tales of the crossing are sure to rekindle the most heated controversy. A three-hundred-foot drop down chimneys, chutes, and narrow-ledged "stairways"—spread-eagled climbing over nearly vertical cliff faces. At times a pair of wings may be desirable, for one false step sends one plummeting a thousand feet down the north face. Many parties desire the security of a rope, although steady hands and some gusto are all one needs to get across.

It felt wrong, but I went along. We couldn't even agree on the descent. The guidebook said to take the first pitch, but from the summit three chutes branched down to the ridge. We took the middle course to my dismay, but only because the others looked just as bad, if not worse.

Gusts of wind made us crouch as we stalked a totally exposed catwalk. The spiny ridge was composed of crumbling, fragmented shale—a veritable sidewalk in the sky in bad need of repair. The first step off was into the worst mistake of my life—a slick, water-worn chute with nothing but pressure handholds and crumbling footrests. I wanted to turn back, but I was the man and I was in front. I could see where I would fall and die. Nothing in the world could save or brace me. Whereas, if my girlfriend slipped or fell at least I would be her second chance.

My heart was pounding. Blood and adrenalin coursing. My hands and lips were tingling from fear. But I felt impatience from behind.

"You can go ahead of me," I half-joked.

"No, no. Take your time. No need to rush. Just be careful."

We inched our way down. The steepness and lack of secure handholds made me wonder whether we were on track. Maybe we should be descending one of the other chutes. But she seemed confident and dauntless, and so I went along.

"Well, if this is the worst it gets then it's not so bad," she encouraged. "We don't have much farther to go."

But it did get worse. The steeply-angled chute suddenly dropped off a nearly vertical cliff. Etched into the crumbling sedimentary shale were naturally worn ledges spaced so evenly that they resembled a man-made stairway.

I began trembling, feeling cold and clammy. My stomach leapt up to my heart and my heart leapt into my throat. Could she even see what we were about to descend?

I steeled myself and cautiously slipped feet first over the ledge. Face forward, back to the wall, an airy thousand foot drop to my death. My backpack brushed and caught along the rocks, determined to push me over the edge. I would have to turn and face the cliff, descending backwards step by step, relying on the blind fumbling and feeling of my feet. I turned and was relieved not to be gazing down into the abyss. I was just as scared, but at least the psychology had changed. Death was more acceptable if it wasn't staring you in the face.

We descended slowly ledge by ledge. Waiting to secure her descent gave me the needed time to catch my breath and regain my composure. For at every step and movement I expected the crumbling ledge to give way. Every moment I was expecting to die.

We made it down the staircase to the top of a forty foot chimney. It was a relief being confronted with a "mere" forty foot drop. For one thing, we could now wedge ourselves down the crack with pressure. For another, if we fell we had a better chance of surviving. I was scared, but I now realized that fear had different degrees. Terror was what I had experienced on the "staircase." I was now breathing more regularly and was more in control.

When climbing in the Borgonian Mountains care should be taken not to become over-confident. On September 21st Vaughn Youngs fell to his death when a ledge he was standing on suddenly gave way. The veteran climber had successfully scaled Desolation six times in the past. Witnesses claim the incident as merely a freak accident. "Vaughn was so confident and sure of himself—he couldn't have done anything wrong." But just as lack of confidence hampers and impedes natural abilities, so too can over-confidence. Fear naturally inspires caution, whereas lack of fear can lead to carelessness. In the Borgonian Mountains a fine line of confidence exists. Its lack can kill through timidity and hesitance. Its excess can kill through taking things for granted.

We made it down to the bottom of the chimney. Not much farther to go. We inched our way precariously along a horizontal cliff ledge. Our backpacks, the force of gravity, all conspiring to tip us off the teetering edge. I stopped after twenty feet, not because I wanted to, but because I had to. There was nowhere to go. The ledge had disappeared and what confronted me was a sheer vertical face of rock. I looked around to see where I had gone wrong.

"Maybe we took the wrong approach," I suggested in bafflement and horror.

"We couldn't have," she argued. "Besides, this is exactly the way it's described. Only fifteen more feet and then we're free."

"All right," I said in warning, "if you're sure you want to go through with it."

I could surely make it across if she was so determined. We would just have to be careful and take a deep breath. I wondered if she had thoroughly read the guidebook. Did she know what she was getting into? Did she really want to go across? But this obviously wasn't the time to scare her with warnings. What was needed now was confidence and inspiration.

The last challenge of the Desolation Traverse is the deceptive fifteen foot cliff face. Once across, it is smooth sailing over the ridge and up to the peak. But those alluring fifteen feet are the most deadly. Over half the fatal accidents occur at this spot. It is the point of decision-making, the point of turning back. The spread-eagle clinging is facilitated by what technical climbers consider to be the best rock in the country—a climber's paradise—large knobs of conglomerate perfect for grabbing or standing upon.

From the ledge I reached out one hand to arm's length and grabbed hold of a conglomerate knob. It was a perfect handhold—an immovable concretion that filled my grasp. My other hand was still clinging to the ledge, stretching me to the limit. My next move was clearly to let go and begin my spread-eagle, hand-over-hand, foot-by-foot scramble across the cliff. But my hand wouldn't let go of the safe, secure ledge. I wanted to let go, but my hand knew better. In fact it did the opposite and tightened its grip.

I looked down to where I would fall and now I myself didn't want to let go. My heart was pounding. I was trembling and gasping for air. My muscles felt like sponges and I was breaking into a cold sweat. Did I know what I was getting into? Did I really want to go across? Once started I would be committed. I would have to go all the way. For turning around on a vertical wall was almost impossible.

I had to calm down because I was verging on panic. I had to have time to think, to reconsider my options.

"What's wrong?" she asked as I was motionless for so long. I was paralyzed by a fear that had to be conquered.

"Nothing," I feigned calmly, "just plotting out how to get across."

"Stay calm," I consoled myself as I would a novice. "Take a deep breath and relax. You have all the time in the world. Just be careful and test each rock before committing your weight. Take it slow and easy and look across, not down." I looked down and almost fainted. "Remember, in order to traverse you must let go. Now ease your grip on the ledge. That's it, just let go and reach out for another knob. Don't worry. You're doing fine. Just relax, take a deep breath, and on the count of three let go. One—oh my god, my heart was pounding, throbbing. Two—my life was passing before me. I could see my fall—the headlines—the foolishness of the act. Three—I released my grasp, closed my eyes, crossed over. The passing, the ending, the never turning back. The dream fades, was never there. I open my eyes to the emptiness. My love, my all and everything—a figment of my mind ..."

MISSING CLIMBER

The week-long search for a missing climber was called off early this morning. Heavy fog hampered visibility and periodic storms made rescue efforts too dangerous. One volunteer of the Mountain Search and Rescue was seriously injured Tuesday afternoon from a fall he sustained on the Desolation knife-edge.

The search for Adrian Landau, the missing climber, began when he failed to arrive at his place of employment (Bob's Donut Shoppette) on Monday morning. A friend said Adrian had acted strange and distant. "He said he was going off for a weekend hike to purge his mind. I never suspected that he would be climbing alone, and never something as dangerous as the knife-edge."

Landau was an experienced climber, having scaled nearly every fourteen thousand plus mountain in the world. His abandoned car was located at the Desolation trailhead. Hikers in the vicinity claimed to have seen strange, glowing lights Sunday night atop Deadman's Traverse. Authorities are puzzled by this development since, at the time, the search and rescue had not yet begun.

STORY-BRIDGE

How we made it across I am unable to recall. For me it is lost in delirium and vague dreams. All I know is that Adrian and I had somehow gained the traverse. We were now standing on the other side of the ravine looking back over the collapsing snow bridge, watching crumbling ice ledges crash and tumble into the gorge.

Neenan Crossing is no more. The traverse no longer exists. The kung-fu members are cleanly severed from both the expedition and from Pochen Point. While Adrian and I can no longer return home to our past.

SEPARATION

Bruce and Lee stand opposite, separated by a void, a chasm impossible to traverse. There is nothing we can do. Fate has split us apart. Only half the expedition can continue on to Pochen Point. The remainder must attempt a return to base camp. It is the only way possible to salvage their lives.

We stand helplessly at the brink not knowing what to do, realizing in our hearts that our paths will never again intertwine. The kung-fu members are self-sacrificing and magnanimous in their gestures.

"See you later," they say cheerfully, bowing deeply, sincerely.

Adrian and I sadly wave good-bye. We stand watching the gradual dissolution of the expedition—Bruce and Lee playfully punching each other as they scamper up and over the rocks. Vanished dreams, lost friendships—but though we have parted externally, in our hearts we never will.

Those comic, dueling antagonists—they did everything and never complained. And though they were turning back, I knew they had already attained their goal of Pochen Point, because Pochen Point was really within them.

THE SPECTACLE

Near the rendezvous we come upon evidence of the spectacle. Atop Sanchan Needle I look down onto a sea of billowing, white clouds. Before me an enormous arc arches up out of the mist. It is like a rainbow, but foggy white, and it stretches across the entire valley. In all my mountaineering I have never seen its likes before. What is it? What does it mean? An omen? A vision? I watch in amazement as the milky band seems to convulse and pulsate. Is it imagination or is there a subtle hissing in the air?

As if this were not supernatural enough, a darkness begins forming beneath the ghostly halo. The shadow shapes into gargantuan proportions—a monster, a demon, a giant human form emerges. Is it the legendary god of the Yeti? Is it the ghost of Tensing?

A moment later Adrian arrives by my side. At the same moment a second giant forms under the halo. I wave my arms and one of the enormous silhouettes also waves its arms. It is me. The awesome fear—Tensing, the Yeti. The mystic vision is really myself.

RENDEZVOUS AT BEAR'S PLAYGROUND

One Small Step For Man

The expedition (comprised solely of Adrian and me) recovers its composure, accepts what is fate, rendezvous at its appointed destiny—Pochen Pass. To our astonishment Dave has returned with Bob. But Bob is weak and delirious and, according to Adrian, he is dying. Bob mumbles incoherently, yet the tone, though resigned and tired, is nevertheless still happy. One Mad Climber, at least, has met his dream.

THE LAST PITCH

At the Bears' Playground the remains of the expedition encamps on Day 107. From the saddle—a broad, lichen-covered plateau—the peak looms enticingly and forebodingly in the distance. It is obvious where our path lies. Up the steep, red couloir and over the north ridge to the summit. Hard work, but after what we've been through, really child's play—a long day's hike.

However, on turning to my companions I am horrified by a sudden suspicion. Adrian is gazing off to a peak on the left. Dave is surveying the knife-edge to the south. Bob is resting slumped over on the ground. Fellow travelers for life!—what was going wrong? We were almost there. We were almost to the top.

Camp is made as quickly as our exhaustion allows. Fingers are frozen, lack of oxygen makes every movement a feat. Bob lies curled up in his bag panting for air.

"We looked everywhere for the way," he gasps, "but where it really was—within." He tries to laugh and breaks into a fit of choked coughing instead.

We huddle around to give him our warmth, hold his hand to let him know we are there—a night vigil, a living wake.

But when the morning dawns he is no longer there.

"Tensing?"

"Yes, Master."

"Are we there yet?"

"You've always been there."

THE DISTINGUISHED
WHITE SASH

DISSOLUTION

The body is exposed and eviscerated—broken down so as to be more easily assimilated. There is no remorse, no argument. Each one knows the way he must go. We break camp—burn and bury the essentials. There was no more use, no more need.

How much was weariness, altitude sickness, or dream? The expedition parts nevertheless at first light on Day 108. Each member traveling his separate way. In the half-light atop Pochen Plateau three dark silhouettes move gradually apart—each heading for what he takes as the Point. Was it different for each man? Was Pochen Point only a figment of the imagination? A subjective exploration. A path. A state of mind?

We climb all the same merely accepting without question.

PASSAGE

I climb without thinking—because it is the only way I can go. There is no return. The past is a dream. Upwards, forwards, onwards to my fate. The movement, the passage, yearning to be complete.

The words echo and resound through my being. "It is not the goal that matters, but simply the path." The expedition—was it simply the journey through life? And where was I now? Where had it taken me? But it was the process, the living, the experience that made the difference. The goal was superfluous, the way was paramount.

"Yet some say that what matters is not even the path, but rather the passage—the pathless path."

ACCEPTANCE

Step by step my life flashes before me. Childhood faces in a playground. Family outings. First loves. Only now, when it is irrevocable, do I understand the significance of my past. I see clearly how each moment, each movement could have been different. One small turn and everything could have changed. But somehow it no longer matters. I have no regrets.

TRANSCENDENCE

A hundred feet from the top. The summit gleams red-orange in the alpenglow of the setting sun. Pochen Point. The goal of life. The summit of the nether world. Had I assumed more than I could handle? Would I ever reach the top? Each step is a painful struggle. Every breath a labored tearing in my lungs. Wheezing. Gasping. Coughing up blood. The shadow of encroaching dusk follows me to the crest, chasing me, prodding, urging me toward my goal. Would I make it in time? Would I reach Pochen Point before dark? The shadows advance from below, chilling the air. But the point up ahead still burns with golden light.

Fifty feet to summit. Darkness closing. Nearly there. Trudging step by step on rubbery legs. Stumbling and falling. Pulling myself to the top. The expedition. The goal. The purpose. At last . . .

The last step. For a moment bathed in warm, golden alpenglow. Basking in the radiance of the setting sun—dying embers refusing to burn out. But fading in the cold darkness. A vanishing beacon in the night. A struggle. A play of light. It is the way of life. Of aeons . . . of eternities. The meaning of life—to be—transcended . . .

Unbeknownst to them, Tensing's party was purportedly the first and last expedition ever to have attained Pochen Point. With them the gap closed forever.

www.ingramcontent.com/pod-product-compliance
Lightning Source LLC
Chambersburg PA
CBHW070007260626
47159CB00005B/1712